The 3rd Floor

The 3rd Floor

and other stories of the Portuguese resistance

Manuel Tiago
(Álvaro Cunhal)

Translated and with a foreword by
Eric A. Gordon

INTERNATIONAL PUBLISHERS
New York

First English language edition, 2021 by International Publishers Co., Inc. / NY
by special arrangement with Editorial Avante!

Translated from the Portuguese by Eric A. Gordon © 2020

Printed in the United States of America

Library of Congress Cataloging-in-Publication Data

Names: Tiago, Manuel, author. | Gordon, Eric A., 1945– translator, writer
 of foreword.
Title: The 3rd floor : and other stories of the Portuguese resistance /
 Manuel Tiago (Alvaro Cunhal) ; translated and with a foreword by Eric A.
 Gordon.
Other titles: Sala 3 e outros contos. English | Third floor
Description: First English language edition. | New York : International
 Publishers, 2021. | Summary: "We present these stories in a certain
 order as if to suggest the birth, adventures and day-to-day lives of
 Communist militants in fascist Portugal as portrayed in different
 characters at discrete stages of political evolution"—Provided by
 publisher.
Identifiers: LCCN 2021025737 | ISBN 9780717808717 (paperback)
Subjects: LCSH: Tiago, Manuel—Translations into English. | LCGFT: Short
 stories.
Classification: LCC PQ9282.I23 S2513 2021 | DDC 869.3/42—dc23
LC record available at https://lccn.loc.gov/2021025737

ISBN-10: 0-7178-0871-1   ISBN-13: 978-0-7178-0871-7
Typeset by Amnet Systems, Chennai, India

Table of Contents

Also available from International Publishers
in its series of fictional works by
Manuel Tiago

Five Days, Five Nights
"devoid of the stilted political speechifying sometimes
found in political fiction, the novella manages to capture the
complexities, loneliness, and bravery of ordinary people"
(*Monthly Review*)

The Six-Pointed Star
"a breathtaking novel of heartbreaking vignettes"
(*Culture Matters*)

Foreword

By Eric A. Gordon

IN an interview that *People's World* Managing Editor C.J. Atkins conducted with me when the first of the Manuel Tiago books appeared, "How did Álvaro Cunhal's *Five Days, Five Nights* get its English translation?" (*People's World*, November 17, 2020), he asked me, "So why would readers in English be interested in him? Is he a great world writer who, maybe because of his politics, never got the recognition he deserved?"

Here's what I answered:

"That's a good question! I'll try to answer as honestly as possible—and hope it doesn't hurt book sales! I'm not sure I would say he's a 'great' writer ranked with the brightest luminaries of world literature, but definitely I would say an important writer. I'm going to upstage some possible future critics and reviewers and state my opinion, that Manuel Tiago is uneven in terms of always paying sufficient attention to character development. Even though in some books—like *Five Days, Five Nights*, for example—he shows us his mastery when he sets his mind to it. In a few of his stories, he drifts into some of the standard formulas of Socialist Realism, you know, righteous-thinking, heroic, flawless proletarian leaders who can do no wrong and sacrifice so much, and so thanklessly, for the cause. But in most cases, it's a pretty healthy mix of a profound knowledge of human character, with all our foibles, with the artist's obligation to write about dedicated, optimistic people with a strong sense of purpose.

"But here's why I say he's important, apart from how history will eventually judge him as a literary figure. Because what he writes about is something few others tackle—life under extreme conditions of repressive fascist oppression, and how resisters organize and live to see another day. The opposition to Portuguese fascism lasted as long as the regime itself, from 1927 to 1974. How do people survive, how do they act to improve conditions, how do they effect change, how do they deal with setbacks, how do they work from within, how do they pass on the habit and tradition of resistance from generation to generation? I cannot think of another writer who, with such granular attention to the specifics of day-to-day clandestine party work, lays out through their collected oeuvre such a vast collective portrait of a whole nation in struggle against such entrenched evil. There is a great deal that is pleasurable to read in his work from the storytelling point of view, but beyond that, his work is instructive and illuminating for the whole process of resistance in whatever country at any time."

At the time I came up with that answer I had recently completed work on the volume you are holding in your hands now. My description of Manuel Tiago's importance reflects precisely—in my view, of course—what the reader will find in this collection of stories. From a literary point of view, it is uneven. (Helluva way to introduce the first publication of these stories in English!) But I do not wish to make claims for Tiago's work that the reader will find inflated and unjustified.

Just speaking personally, though readers are free to differ with me, I find the characterizations of the principal figures in the first and third stories here somewhat underdeveloped. We don't really get deep enough into the sinews of these young men—Miguel in "An Uncommon Education" and Leonel in "Struggle and Life"—to figure out what motivates them, nor whence that impetus comes, nor why the women in their lives find them (at least for a time) suitable partners.

My literary reservations may have their roots in another explanation. The model of the stalwart political cadre who unquestioningly answers his party's call for whatever assignment or task may be laid on him is almost everywhere now a thing of the past. One may forcefully, and perhaps correctly argue that the extreme conditions of fascism dictated a strict vertical system of command if the project of resistance were to be effective—which, of course, it eventually was. There can be no disputing that it was this structure of severe discipline that kept the Portuguese Communist Party intact for all those long years and made it the opposition's leading force. One can only stand back in reverent admiration and gratitude toward those Party members who sacrificed virtually every personal pleasure in life—in some cases life itself—for the greater cause. It's just that there are hardly any parties like that anymore, and few people who would submit themselves, according to our modern sensibilities, to such almost cult-like regimentation.

The fact that Tiago brings us into that clandestine world, so closely, so intimately, and leaves for us the legacy of that time and the demands it made on committed militants, outweighs—for me—any perceived literary lapses. If the time should ever come, anywhere, when this level of organized underground resistance is called for, then pick up these books and study how it was once done.

Having said which, these stories are engaging in their own ways, and Tiago introduces us to some memorable characters and scenes. One minor but interesting detail in "Struggle and Life" is a reference to a character who had spent a short spell at Aljube Prison in Lisbon which, from the description, seems to be the unnamed prison of the previous story, "The 3rd Floor." For the sake of clarification, Aljube is not the main penitentiary with 500 prisoners portrayed in Tiago's *The Six-Pointed Star*, which was the second release in the Manuel Tiago series.

Another point in "Struggle and Life" illustrates once again the strong autobiographical source for many details in Tiago's writing. The escaped prisoner Alexandre is harbored in a safe house in the town of Achada in the Mafra area. When Álvaro Cunhal escaped from the Fort of Peniche prison in early 1960, that is exactly where he was taken. A photo of that house is included on p. 81 of the *Álvaro Cunhal Fotobiografia* published by Avante! in 2013 for Cunhal's centennial.

The other two stories, "The 3rd Floor" and "The Vargas Case: Death of a Landowner," carry a somewhat different valence, not so dominated by the Socialist Realist esthetic. Both have the virtue, from the reader's point of view, of being suspense stories. In the former, will the daring prison escape be successful? And the last story in the book, more or less a police procedural involving the colorful inhabitants of a small

X   THE 3RD FLOOR

village in an agricultural district, is Tiago's wholly successful, and often humorous stab at the murder mystery genre.

We present these stories in a certain order as if to suggest the birth, adventures and day-to-day lives of Communist militants in fascist Portugal as portrayed in different characters at discrete stages of political evolution. The presence of the Party is not felt in the last story, at least not overtly, but nevertheless it reflects the collective stance of a rural community toward a generally hated landowner, perhaps indicating how deeply anti-oligarchical ideas have embedded themselves even amongst a non-politically engaged population.

I extend deep thanks to all those who helped by reading this work and offering their suggestions: Bill Gregory, Francisco Melo, Gary Bono, Janice Rothstein, John Mueter, José Oliveira, Kathie Dean, Robert N. Miller, Ruth Judkowitz, Steve Johnson.

The 3rd Floor

A view of the Marina Grande Train Station

An Uncommon Education

1

LIFE was quiet on North Street, a narrow road stretching against the slope of a hill, with little traffic and rarely anyone parking there.

The modest Pereira house was like the others, just more spacious. On the street level, a door and three windows in front, a central corridor ending in an informal space that served as kitchen, dining room, living room and visiting room.

The family was small: António, a metal worker, his wife Conceição, and two daughters, Ester, an office worker, and Sofia, a student.

The grandmother had died after prolonged suffering. She had stopped talking. Everyone helped her in her slow agony, especially Ester, who left her previous job for this, and with her mother, cared for her all day long. The sickness reached a point where it was hard to say who suffered more, the patient or the caregiver. Everyone gave their all. Something hard to discern bound Ester to her grandmother, maybe the almost maternal acts of a granddaughter, maybe the good night kiss they shared at bedtime. It was not surprising that in the final moments of her life, it was toward Ester that Grandmother turned her last glance in an unmistakable expression of recognition and tenderness.

After her death, life went on in the house, and little by little the sorrow faded. The married couple had their room, and the two daughters had another. In respectful disuse, the room grandmother had occupied remained closed.

Behind the house, along the incline of the land, they kept a small vegetable garden and flowerbed. The garden had two entrances. One was from the street through the interior of the house. The other was from a trail that led from behind the garden and flowerbed and farther down reached a sharp curve in the road.

Saturdays and Sundays, while the mother attended to domestic chores, the others also worked with pleasurable enthusiasm. Sofia especially liked taking care of the flowerbed, laid out in the colorful harmony of roses, daisies, violets, calla lilies and gladiolas. The gladiolas were her pride, but roses her favorite because of the fragrance.

Ester and their father worked the vegetable patch: Lettuce, tomatoes, cabbage, parsley, and Ester's favorite, sweet-smelling, tasty peppers.

Knee-high Portuguese kale marked the borders of the garden. The only tree was an apricot tree that grew visibly from year to year. For watering they used a long hose attached to the spigot in the kitchen.

Weeding the garden beds, father and daughters breathed deep the healthy aroma of moist earth. On those hot days of summer they believed that to be the freshest and most welcoming spot anywhere in the house. On a break from their work, they found a delicious lunch waiting for them.

Conceição was not just the perfect housekeeper. The kitchen was her forte, and she did not conceal a certain pride she felt over the dishes she prepared, however simple and humble. She received high marks for her bean soup and her red or white beans, her vegetables and her cod stew, to which she lent special flavor with peppers and tomatoes from the garden. And above all was the delicious bouillon whose secret she guarded jealously. No one ever figured out how she made it.

Though they lived in common, their ways of speaking and temperaments were different. António left early for work in a calm state of mind and at a brisk pace, and returned from work with the same calm and assurance.

Conceição spoke little. She'd call out in a loud voice for the others to come to the table. She asked more questions than she made comments.

Like her father, Ester was more given to smiles than to laughter, with sudden reactions that were hard to explain.

Sofia had a somewhat contradictory manner about her. Though happy and talkative, at certain times in conversation with others she'd suddenly turn quiet and reflective.

Family life proceeded smoothly. On their street they were regarded as dignified people, a normal and even exemplary family.

2

As in any village, neighbors on the narrow street greeted each other good morning and good afternoon. Some occasionally dropped by the Pereiras' for brief visits, while others went there more frequently.

That was the case with Laura, who lived in the house facing them. The wife of a seaman, she was alone for weeks on end, and found relief from her solitude at the Pereira household. A longtime friend of the family, they welcomed her as though she were indeed family.

José Pedro, a retired metal worker, visited often. On those hot summer nights, he appeared coming down the street at a slow, natural gait, so punctual that, arriving at his neighbors' door, they opened it immediately because they were expecting him at that exact time.

That was also true of Tó, a lively, uninhibited adolescent who left his own house and entered the house right next door. They liked to kid him. "So, who are you going out with these days?"

"No, no," he protested, irritated. He didn't go there for the girls, but to go back to the patio, breathe the fresh air, and entertain himself watching the ants on their trails and chasing butterflies.

One visitor to the house, to whom they offered special welcome, was the young man Miguel, son of Midões, a peculiar man on the street. In the morning, when he left for work, he walked silently past the house down to the traffic circle, and drove off in the car he had parked there. There were entire days when no one would see him. The neighbors talked, but as time passed they became accustomed to it.

Miguel was very different from his father, however. A friendly boy, he engaged easily with people and went to the Pereira house frequently. A hop and a skip, and he was there.

One day, Laura, as she would also say maliciously to Tó, told him, "You're not fooling anyone, Miguel. Sofia's a pretty girl, don't you think?"

She posed a similar question to Sofia. "Hey, Sofia, anyone can see by your eyes, you like him."

Neither Miguel nor Sofia would confirm or deny it. They just smiled. And smiled, because no one knew that Miguel went to wait for Sofia when she got out of school and they would sit together conversing in the park.

Their talks took increasingly intimate turns. "What do you like most in life, Sofia?"

"I don't know…," she answered. "A lot of things."

"Studying?"

"Yes. But not only what they teach in school. More than anything else, the prospects for children and young people. I worry about the economic shortages for so many, the illnesses badly treated, the lack of means to buy books and toys."

"And dancing?"

"I'm not drawn to it."

One time, the conversation brought out two revelations. He asked, "Would you like to travel? See the world?"

Her answer surprised him. "Not really. I like being at home, living and sharing with my family."

More surprising still was Miguel's response. "You're lucky. In my house I feel alone, completely alone."

Their conversations continued back at the house in front of everyone. They always had things to say to one another. They kissed each other socially, but with restraint, like something fraternal.

Neighbors on the street visited. They all knew each other. There was one exception, however, a young woman, elegantly dressed, with greenish eyes and beautiful black hair. So beautiful that, one time she had come to the house, Ester couldn't resist commenting. "Lila, what beautiful hair you have. It's your hair that gives such character to your face. It would be a shame if you followed the fashion and decided to dye it."

Lila did not answer and put on an inscrutable face.

That was life at the Pereiras'—so quiet, so uneventful, so uniform, and yet, everything instilled with little mysteries. But wasn't it like that in other houses, in other families? Aren't they also full of little mysteries of life, the life and the feelings of everyone, be it Lila, or Sofia or Ester, or any of the most sensible, the most sociable, the most honest, the most transparent, the best of friends out of all your friends? Wasn't that true also of António and the conversations he had with José Pedro well into the night after the others had gone to bed?

The Pereira family, like all the others, harbored its little mysteries. But what was the reason that they attracted all these people to the house for such frank and friendly gatherings? Maybe because they were the most tranquil, most peaceable family on the street, and everyone recognized them as such.

3

Miguel's intimacy with the Pereira family was not to the liking of his father, Midões. At first, they saw him frequently spying on his son, sometimes hiding himself behind a staircase, other times at the street corner, and still other times walking down the street and turning around right away to come back up, surveying everything on both sides.

Choosing the opportune moment, Miguel entered his friends' house, and his father, not having seen him, returned home grumbling to himself. Then things got more complicated.

One day, catching his son on the way to the Pereiras', Midões stopped him, and someone heard him say, in a restrained but violent tone, "You better wise up. You know I don't like and I don't want you visiting those people."

Some days later he stopped him again. "No, I won't have you laughing at me," he growled. And grabbing him with a violent tug on his arm, he dragged him home and violently shoved him around.

The conflict between father and son was commented upon widely. No one knew of anything like it. The tension turned threatening, it hung in the air, and everyone felt fearful that a disaster was coming.

People asked why things had devolved into such a raw state. The Pereiras were an earnest, stable family. The boy was nice and respectful.

For years, the neighbors had gotten accustomed to a man of such strange behavior living amongst them. And if initial curiosity about him had waned over time, his latest violent outbursts toward his son revived old questions and suspicions.

Who was this man, anyway? How could one understand his life? Why did he persecute his son so? And further, what kind of occupation would explain why, from time to time, no one saw him or knew where he was?

Once again, after his latest brutal attacks, Midões disappeared for some time. Observations, questions, comments and fears re-emerged.

What did this man do, after all? Why did he keep himself apart from everyone? How come the woman who lived with him so seldom spoke with the neighbors, and never said hello to anyone? Who was he, and what did he do for a living?

Laura had her own theory: That Midões was a major drug dealer and feared that his son might spill the beans on him. "You might not believe it," she insisted, "but it's as clear as water. And you know I'm never wrong—"

"If it's clear as water," José Pedro interrupted, "it's muddy water."

"Yes, muddy water, very muddy," Laura agreed. "But if it's not that, then what is it?"

Since Miguel continued to visit the Pereiras, although now with greater caution, what would the father's reaction be if he caught him again? Everyone felt anxious that a tragedy was approaching.

And it did.

Discovering his son once again on his way to his friends' house, he roared, took hold of him, dragged him down the street to the door of his house, and threw him face-forward against the front wall. Once, twice, three times. His face all bloody, the boy collapsed almost unconscious.

After a hot day, neighbors were taking a stroll on the sidewalk in the cool evening air. They witnessed the scene and went running to help.

Outraged, they saw Midões through the lighted window, pacing back and forth as if nothing had happened.

In an uproar from the street, some yelled, "Assassin! Assassin!"

Laura and others picked up and propped up the wounded boy. José Pedro took him in his arms.

In a cortege, they lifted him through the streets, to the sound of shouting, a march of ghosts. The group paid attention to nothing around them, only living in their pain and the immediate goal of where they were taking him. Passersby, in a mixture of surprise and respect, didn't presume to ask what had happened.

The marchers hurried along the long route, and left the wounded man in the care of the emergency room at the hospital. Since no one asked them anything, no one volunteered anything, and that was that.

Still in intensive care, Miguel experienced terrible pain on his lacerated face for several days—days of immense suffering: Confusion, hallucination and weakness, loss of consciousness, sleepiness, and waking up suddenly with intense pain and the desire to scream.

Amidst this confused state of consciousness, a few questions struck him like quick, sharp, aggressive lightning bolts of lucidity.

Why that ferocious aggression? Why from his own father? Why did he hate the Pereiras so much? What had he, Miguel, done wrong?

And later, equally confused, fleeting images—of his father's house with the strange lover, the Pereira house, and visions of Sofia.

These questions and images haunted him for long days and nights. After he transferred to the infirmary and got adjusted to his new and congenial surroundings, they persisted, though less frequently and powerfully.

In the meantime, in the days following the attack, suspicious characters passed on the street straight to the Midões house, poking around, looking through windows in an intimidating manner.

During that week, Midões appeared only once, coming up the street. By chance, he tripped, and it took a grotesque, ridiculous effort on his part not to fall flat on the ground.

A youthful laughter rose up. Regaining his balance in a fury, Midões saw a young kid, Tó, running down the street like a rabbit.

4

From urgent care Miguel went to the infirmary, a long hall with two rows of beds squeezed closely together, moans, complaints, shouts, protests and cries, a symphony of pain and suffering.

Over time, one or another patient imposed his presence over the others: A sharp outcry piercing the void; a constant, ceaseless groaning; a repetitious, complaining voice reciting his bad luck. "She told me plainly, told me straight out, and I didn't want to hear her. She told me plainly…."

So many screams, the same and different. Why the difference between screams of pain, whose pitifulness seems comparable? Because they're not, in fact, comparable? Because they're objectively different? Because of despair in some and courageous restraint in others? Surely, to those who hear it, the first impression is that the most penetrating scream corresponds to the least bearable pain. The infirmary was a chorus of screams, a concert of suffering in the most contrasting of voices.

During treatment hours, echoing throughout the infirmary alongside the desperate howls and complaints from so many sick and wounded people, there were also sincere words of gratitude that could be heard.

It's surprising that, in an ambience so heavy with sighs, cries and screams, you could also hear jokes and even laughter from people who told funny stories about their lives.

"I was already enlisted," one patient in the next bed recounted, "and do you know how they put me out of the service at the military hospital? You don't know, right? It was because of a clove of garlic—"

"Garlic?"

"Yes, garlic. If you place a clove of garlic way up your ass, it's like you're having an attack of bilious fever."

"And?"

"I became all yellow, the color of tincture of iodine. The doctors examined me and observed me, and decided I was incapacitated for military service."

"I was a soldier, too," another started, "and because of the smallest thing I did *not* get out of the army. You know how?" Anticipatory silence followed.

"For you, it was thanks to a clove of garlic. For me, it was thanks to a bread crumb."

Laughter broke out. "Liar! You're joking."

"Me, joking? I'll tell you. I went to the medic on my unit, a captain stupid as a toad, and I complained of violent pains in my stomach. They took me to the hospital and did an X-ray. And that's where the breadcrumb enters the story. I had swallowed a bite of dry bread, it wasn't easy, but I did. They took the image and they were shocked. The spot presented no doubt. It was a huge ulcer."

"But you said you *didn't* get out—"

"Right, I didn't, and you know why? If I had swallowed a smaller piece it would have gone down. But what they saw was so extraordinary they decided to do another X-ray. That's when it all started falling apart. The ulcer spot was much smaller, and it had changed position—"

"And then?"

"And then it cost me two weeks of disciplinary detention."

By contrast to these high-spirited patients, others told their sad stories, hard to tell if they were true or false.

"She hated men," one patient declared. Doubtfully, another man shrugged his shoulders, so the storyteller continued.

"She wound up hating men forever." And with that, his narrative took flight.

Still in school, as a young girl, a teacher grabbed her alone, attacked her from the rear, took hold of her arms, and kissed her so brutally that, just recalling it, the girl developed profound nausea and the urge to vomit.

"You're inventing it," someone interrupted.

"Inventing?" the narrator said indignantly. "If you don't want to listen, don't listen, but this is what happened."

The girl thought that if a kiss was the repugnant taste of that fresh spit, she never again wanted to kiss a man, and concluded that men are monsters.

"Not all that much to get so worked up about," commented someone off to the side. "The girl must have been a hysteric."

"You don't think so? You think it was so insignificant? All I can say is, if it was my daughter, I would have killed the guy. And you know what else—"

Neither the funny stories nor the sad tales changed the atmosphere. At every moment the infirmary reasserted its own reality. The story was interrupted by piercing screams—maybe an especially painful treatment, or maybe unbearable suffering.

That was the infirmary to which they had brought Miguel.

His suffering was intense. He couldn't find a comfortable position lying down. The lacerations on his face caused him terrible pain. He tried to sleep, but sleep rebelled against him. It fled arrogantly, farther and farther away, stubbornly refusing for infinite stretches of time to respond to the wounds' call for relief. Until finally, as quick as eagle dives, it did answer the call and led the injured man into the deep calm and sweet serenity of sleep—the moment he had been anxiously awaiting all day.

5

The worsening condition of his wounds led to Miguel's transfer to a narrow operating chamber where they subjected him to delicate surgical intervention. A few days later, the doctor explained, "These two ladies will be taking care of you. They're among the most competent and dedicated we have."

The doctor's words were true. The two nurses treated him extremely attentively and efficiently: Cláudia and Emília. Emília, now in her forties, was reserved and spoke little. Cláudia was young and beautiful, happy and outgoing.

From the beginning, they asked the inevitable questions. The people who had brought the injured boy to the hospital had only said that Miguel had been the victim of an assault.

Cláudia and Emília wanted to know more about that mystery, not out of idle curiosity, but out of interest in this unusual case. Little by little, today one, the next day another, the questions arose naturally, almost unavoidably. Who had attacked him? Who had put him into a state like that? A stranger? Another boy? Where did it happen, and for what reason?

Miguel didn't answer, not even when they pushed him. His silence unsettled them, and only increased the nurses' bewilderment and anger, especially Cláudia's. One day she couldn't hold herself back. "The savage who did this to you deserves to be in prison—or else someone should do it to him."

The calmly self-possessed Emília agreed. Prison, yes, but not to be the victim of the same cruel attack. Cláudia repeated herself with unexpected fervor: Yes, he deserved for someone to do it to him. Was there a worse crime than destroying the face of a young man as sweet and handsome as this one?

The tone of this remark prompted Emília's instantaneous concern. "Cláudia, Cláudia, keep your emotions under control."

The time had come for controlling them.

Now, every time Miguel finished a treatment, she began making a fuss of grooming his hair. What harm could come of such caresses? A profound bond was forming that was hard to describe. Words followed gestures. "We want to make you well the soonest possible, but I'll be sorry to see you go."

Her words turned evermore transparent, and evermore removed from reality. "I will miss you, you know?"

She wanted him to heal, but at heart, that he not go away.

Miguel's words also took on the same tone. That being here with her was a gift he wouldn't want to lose. That he had never experienced such moments that made him feel so alive.

"I never imagined I would meet a girl like you, wounded in a hospital."

"And I," Cláudia responded, "never imagined I would have a patient I would feel such affection for."

So between the two of them an abiding, loving connection was born and grew. Daydreams blossomed into bursts of spontaneous emotion. That they couldn't accept the idea of never seeing one another again. That they could meet, after he left there: dreams rising and disappearing, always intense, alive and contradictory.

Strange, but during those weeks spent in recovery, Miguel, enchanted with Cláudia, with her beauty and tenderness, never even remembered Sofia. Hard to believe, but it was the pure truth, one he would later, in embarrassment, struggle with.

After a month they took him back to the infirmary. There, at visiting hours, he received his friends. Laura brought him, with some delicious cookies, her dear friendship.

But in the noisy tumult of the visiting families, the unexpected visit from Sofia, whom he had forgotten during the month in the surgery department experiencing the powerful attraction to Cláudia, brought him not happiness, but confusion. Above all, confusion of feelings when, in such contrast to their meetings after school and in the Pereira house, Sofia approached him almost running and, avoiding touching the incisions now only starting to scar over, quickly, tenderly kissed him on his head—a long and loving kiss.

It would have been the happiest moment of Miguel's life, were it not for the image of Cláudia and her smile, her joyousness, her beauty, that willfully dominated his mind.

"I really like you," Sofia murmured.

"We both like each other," Miguel struggled to correct her.

There they were, almost as if they had nothing to say, until the nurses announced the close of visiting hours. Sofia didn't take her leave before giving him another kiss.

It was at that precise moment that Cláudia passed by. Miguel was seized with extreme consternation. He wanted to explain to the one and to the other what he felt for them, his pain and shame for what seemed a double and simultaneous betrayal. And, oh, that rapid glance from Cláudia that was so, so sad. And the surprised, mortified look from Sofia, not presuming anything, but discerning the sensibilities revealed in those brief seconds.

6

A few days later, while Miguel was receiving treatment, Cláudia let him know, in a low voice, that two agents of the PIDE had come to the hospital asking about him. The PIDE was the Polícia Internacional e de Defesa do Estado, or International and State Defense Police. "Make him well quick," they ordered, "and we'll come to fetch him. We have some accounts to settle with him."

"What did you do?" she asked nervously. "Are they following you for politics?"

He laughed. Politics, him? He'd never thought about it. No, not him. He had no idea why they had come looking for him.

"Those are terrible people. One day they could pick you up and kill you."

After another few days, Cláudia expressed herself more clearly. "I'm sorry you'll be leaving, but it would be best if you escaped from here as soon as possible."

Emília was even more insistent. "You have to, my friend."

The plan decided, it was now a question of realizing it. Cláudia asked him, "If you're prepared for it, we'll help you."

The task was not easy. The more they thought and imagined some plan, the more difficult it seemed to bring about. Where would he safely exit? With what clothes? How would he evade unwelcome encounters?

From the rushed expediting of his treatment, and from the way they attended the lesions only beginning to scar, it was obvious that the two nurses were committed to helping him. One new and important problem arose. "Do you have somewhere to go?" Cláudia asked. Days afterward, she added, "We can arrange shelter for you."

By her tone, and her caring eyes, which had become so loving, Miguel believed Cláudia was in fact offering to take him home to her house.

Doubt and confusion besieged him. Accept or not accept? Two crazy and irreconcilable ideas took hold of him: one, accept the offer, the other, to leave the hospital and walk through the streets all night and seek out Sofia at the entrance to her school. One or the other. Or neither.

"Do you have somewhere to go?" Cláudia asked again, appearing disappointed and crushed by his silence in the face of her previous offers. She continued, "Leaving here is no problem. You'll come with us. Then, if you want, I'll take you to a secure place. But you have to decide and tell me in plenty of time."

The next morning, with a sad face, she changed her tone. "I can see that you don't trust us. It's too bad. We could have helped you escape from here and you'd have somewhere to stay. But as it is, we'll get you out, but the rest is up to you."

In those last days, Cláudia showed signs of an unexpected peacefulness. She seemed accepting of the inevitable and natural separation. Her slight peevishness hardly seemed out of place, or so it appeared to Miguel when, half serious and half playfully, she said, "Before you go, I want to give you a kiss. I have the right, don't you think?"

A strange and pointless question, for wasn't it a standard thing to kiss your friends when you saw them? Didn't he kiss Laura? Didn't he kiss Sofia? Why refuse Cláudia, so friendly and caring?

What Miguel still did not know was that a kiss comprises an infinity of varieties, endless meanings, pleasures and tastes beyond imagining. That a kiss could be cordial, but cold. Or could be merely tolerated. It could draw forth resistance and rejection.

What could Miguel know of a kiss of love, when at the cinema the mere simulation of lips touching gave rise to lewd whistling from the balcony? Up to now, Sofia's kisses had been, on the one hand an indication of tenderness, and on the other a conflicted sign of hesitation, lack of confidence, even at times indifference.

He was totally unprepared for Cláudia. Saying goodbye, she carefully held Miguel's head, her lips lightly brushed his, once and again, without haste, in a growing need to satisfy her own pleasure, and finally, as natural as life itself, a deep, never imagined kiss that took possession of his whole body in a powerful conquest of understanding and delight.

In brief seconds, the revelation of a new reality rich with possibility opened up to Miguel.

Life would go on, but never would he forget that passionate kiss, Cláudia's kiss.

With his new clothes on, Miguel was led casually, with the most natural air about him, out the employee exit door. Emília and Cláudia accompanied him a few steps behind, ready to intervene.

Unfortunately, he found himself amidst a clutch of employees who easily recognized him from the infirmary. "So, they've released you?" asked one amazed employee.

"Yes, finally they have," he answered.

"Ah!" the woman reacted in surprise.

They pushed ahead. Bad luck: At the hospital exit, two PIDE agents recognized him.

"So, little pigeon, you wanted to escape? Come with us. We've been waiting for you a long time."

7

Walking the depressing corridors of PIDE headquarters, the agents never stopped lobbing insults at him. "Let's go, you little bastard," said one, "and what's this about you disobeying your daddy?"

"Go on," the other said. "We're going to show you some samples of our product. Just some samples, it was your daddy who recommended us." The two laughed.

They arrived at a small office. "Come on, show what you have in your pockets. Hurry up, you son of a bitch."

His pockets turned inside out, they found a piece of paper. One of them read it quickly and immediately broke out laughing. "Look at this! Listen to this letter he was carrying in his pocket. It's a little love letter. Listen, listen!"

Father, I see you don't like me. You treat me as if I were your worst enemy. I will never return to that house.

"Oh, but you'll return all right. Where else can you go?" one agent said.

"Daddy is waiting for you there," added the other.

Shoving him along, they brought him to another, badly lit room. "Sit down, sit down, you shitty brat you, you must rest."

Miguel sat down, and as the time passed, he waited for what would happen next. He waited and waited an immeasurable time. An uncontrollable urge to sleep lowered him slowly into aching unconsciousness.

A rude slap woke him. He saw an agent's thin, severe face. "What the hell is this, you dickhead? We offered you a chair to rest, and you go fall asleep? In a bed is where you sleep. In a chair you stay awake."

An hour? Two hours? More? Again, sleepiness, and a sad, unconquerable sleep. Suddenly, with his head bowed down, a glass of cold water entered the opening of his shirt and his body broke out in goosebumps.

And when again he nodded off to sleep, he awoke with a scream, his only one during his torture sessions with the PIDE. The agent had held one arm down and put out his cigarette butt on the back of Miguel's hand. The agent had a round face and glasses with thick dark frames, surely relieving the earlier agent.

So he spent the night; the whole night, they wouldn't let him sleep. By morning he was trembling convulsively with cold. His burned hand was most uncomfortable.

Another endless hour more, and the desire for a hot drink was so great that he committed the error of asking for one. "Don't say we're bad folks," said a newcomer who, from his attitude, might have been the chief of the unit. And he offered him a glass of water so freezing that Miguel was incapable of drinking it.

"A shame you don't want it, shithead," the agent said, turning the glass over onto him. "You would have been refreshed for the dance that awaits you."

In a spacious room, a circle of agents were waiting for him. "Look who it is. The son of his daddy."

He had barely heard these words when he received a powerful punch in the stomach: The impact of a heavy fist made him double over in distress and halted his breathing. Then, from all sides he got a brutal beating from one after another. Wielding heavy wooden rods and billy-clubs, they furiously pummeled his whole body. One young agent, with a thin, almost boyish face, brandishing a thick stick, leveled a beating of particular violence, like a madman, ending the series with a sock on the face that was still healing from his earlier wounds.

"Not there," the chief of the unit scolded, and laughed.

But they weren't finished yet. He had fallen on the floor, nearly fainting. They stretched him out, removed his shoes, and struck him dully on the soles of his feet, which sent a shock of terrifying intensity up to the nape of his neck.

"That's enough for a demonstration," said the one who appeared to be in command to his beardless colleague, who kept up his beating in a paroxysm of hysteria, rage and hate.

Finally, they dragged him to a cell and tossed him onto the bunk.

"Sleep a little, because tomorrow there'll be more," said the PIDE agent who led him there.

They closed the door with the metallic sound of the bolt. Miguel lay in complete darkness. Sleep, faint, nightmare? How much time? The sound of the bolt and the door opening. The expressionless face of a guard, his arm extended holding out a bread crust, the door closing and the sound of the bolt. He slept.

He awoke to the indifferent face of another PIDE agent in front of him. "Sorry to have awakened you, asshole. Get out. We still have a few little samples to show you."

Once again he was in the small room. "Stand up and face the wall, and don't move."

Maybe ten minutes, maybe half an hour, his body aching, time without end. Not bearing it any longer, he tried to turn around.

"Turn to the wall, or would you like to go back to the dance?"

He stood for hours, maybe one, maybe two or even three, until he collapsed to the floor. Kicking him, the agent lifted him up brusquely and leaned him against the wall in his former position. "It's only for a few more minutes, and then we'll leave it at that. It was your daddy who recommended giving you just a demonstration. If you ever come back here, we'll give you the whole treatment."

Those last minutes were awful. Three more times he fell, three more beatings.

"Fine, now you'll sleep a bit. We don't want you going out to the street falling down fainting and giving us more work."

He threw himself, shaking, on top of the bunk, and as soon as they closed and bolted the door, he covered himself with the smelly blanket and, half dead, slept deeply.

He had no idea how many hours he was there. Only when they led him through the corridors and staircases did he see that dusk was falling. In a wider corridor a tall, beefy man was leaning on a wall waiting for them.

"Good evening, senhor inspector. The service is completed."

The inspector kept them standing and spoke in a calm, affected voice, directing himself to the detainee. "Listen well and don't forget what I'm about to tell you. As they have told you, you have seen only a small demonstration." After a pause, he continued. "Don't come back here. It would be best for you. Forget the letter that we found in your pocket, go home and beg forgiveness from your father. Everything will be all right. We know that."

Miguel did not listen to the inspector's counsel. An irrepressible smile lit up his face.

"This guy's an idiot," the inspector remarked.

Miguel's smile, however, came from an unimaginable place. If the inspector could guess it, he would be astonished. Miguel's thought at that moment had nothing to do with the advice to return to his father's house, but instead spelled a strong appeal to life, to the future, to the will to survive, to love and joy. Who knows why at that instant, but floating to his mind was the memory of that unforgettable goodbye kiss from Cláudia.

Still baffled by that smile, they escorted him to the door of the building and, shoving and kicking him out, they hurled him like a piece of garbage onto the street.

A few days later, an agent went to Midões's house. He related what had taken place and showed him the letter Miguel had written him that was found in his pocket.

"And now?" the agent asked.

"That letter says it all," Midões answered. "He doesn't want to return here and I, too, don't want him here." Then, after a slight hesitation, he continued. "You wouldn't want to know any more about him. He's worthless. It's like he doesn't exist. Let the devil take him. He's on his own now."

8

Thrown to the street with kicks and shoves, in pain and unsteady, Miguel didn't know what to do, nor where to take cover. Heading directly to the Pereiras would be dangerous for everyone. So why hadn't he accepted Cláudia's offer? He'd now be in the comfort of a house and perhaps with that beautiful, caring girl at his side looking after him.

In his state of torpor, now he saw Sofia, the school, the garden, their talks, her visiting him in the hospital and placing a long, loving kiss on his head; and now came that irrepressible recollection, superimposing itself on everything else with its own living, actual, appealing reality, of Cláudia's farewell kiss.

He ascended to António Maria Cardoso Street, passed Chiado Square, and suddenly, immersed in the little byways of the district, he completely and utterly lost all notion of the place he found himself in. He wandered randomly from street to street without knowing where he was nor where he was going.

Anxiously, he made a constant, aggressive effort to free himself from the grip of forgetfulness in the face of the unknown, but in vain. The more he tried to break free, the more consummate his disorientation.

In the silence of the night's deserted streets, he saw not a soul. A tenuous fog and the dying light of the street lanterns accentuated his confusion in this part of the city where he stumbled around. Where was he? Where was he going? Where—to where?

The night humidity made his lacerated face, with the still unhealed scars, hurt even more. Extreme fatigue took hold of him, and an urge to flee the confusion that beset him. And while sunken in the dark depth of disorientation, yet there gradually emerged out of his weakness a new, invasive feeling of revolt. Against what he was experiencing? Against himself? Surely, unquestionably, against his inability to free himself from the anguished tension that gripped him in his totally deranged condition. It seemed he was alone and abandoned, living in an unreal world. Evermore dazed and removed from reality, he felt all his strength failing. He was wracked by paralyzing impatience and powerful despair. It was hard to explain: He had two coinciding and equally frustrating feelings—of completely not knowing where he was, and also the tortured futility of ever regaining his presence of mind.

He continued walking without destination, aimless and bewildered. How long? How many hours?

All of a sudden, like a stroke of lightning, he regained consciousness. The suffocating fog of anguish broke, he felt freed finally from the grip of the unknown, and the old city streets reappeared as he had known them. His bright, liberating sense of recognition had come back—of places, houses, the fountain, the unmistakable identity of the district so distinct from any other in the city. It was a clear dawn, and people were already moving about on their way to work.

Finally, having straggled around in haphazard circles, he hadn't got far from the streets he knew. Like a sleepwalker in his last and longest exertion, he made his way to North Street.

Half-crazed, he stood in front of Laura's house. He still wondered if he could find shelter with the Pereiras, but the danger ruled out that idea and he decided on Laura.

"Come in, son. I was almost expecting you," said Laura, welcoming him inside.

Seeing his damaged face, his messy hair, his clothes in rags, and his semi-conscious state, she shortly added, "Sit down here and rest. I'll make you some coffee."

Miguel eagerly sucked up the comforting drink, ate some tasty cookies that Laura served him, and felt his strength return a little.

Laura sat next to him. "Where are you coming from, son? What happened to you?" She already knew he had escaped from the hospital, but nothing more.

In a few words, Miguel told how he was seized and tortured by the PIDE and they had thrown him on the street.

"Well," she stopped him, "we'll talk more later. Now you're going to take a bath, change your clothes and get some sleep."

He needn't be concerned about having nothing to wear. The closet was filled with her husband's clothes and, if he were here, he'd be the first to give him whatever he needed.

Much at ease now, as soon as he lay down he fell asleep. When he awoke, it was already afternoon.

"What are you thinking of doing now, son? Where do you think you'll go?"

Embarrassed, he thought for a moment that Laura did not want him to stay there in her house.

"It would be dangerous to go to the Pereiras' house. Otherwise—"

"—it would be nonsense!" Laura interjected. "Don't you want to stay here in this house until you come up with a better plan?"

The next morning Laura went shopping. When she returned, she found Miguel edgy and irritated.

"I can't bear to be stuck here just waiting and doing nothing," he said as soon as she walked in. He wouldn't and couldn't take it. It was too much.

"Take it easy, son," Laura tried to calm him down. "Be patient." She placed her purchases in the kitchen and came back with a smile. "I'll give you work. You can help me. You'll wash and clean the dishes and help me straighten up the house. Agreed?"

Miguel had calmed down and actually smiled at that thought. "Agreed."

But the very next day he encountered a new cause for impatience. As their usual custom on summer evenings, the residents of North Street sat outside, on the sidewalk, and gossiped. Or they opened their windows and sat there enjoying the fresh air and watching the street.

José Pedro stayed around until late at night, many times the last to leave. So late that the last ones on the street to retire wondered about him. "What kind of business is he up to?" some asked. He was always the last one to return home.

Miguel took notice of these summer nights on the street and exploded. "Can't I at least open the window and take in a little air?" he asked moodily. "I can't take being locked up like this in a jail. What harm would there be breathing a little fresh air?"

"Don't even think about it, son. Everyone knows my husband is still out to sea. If anyone saw you here in the house, they'd want to know if my husband was back, or who else it was living here. People are good, but we have our busybodies."

As she did every day, Laura went over to the Pereira house. Trying to ease their minds about Miguel's situation, for they only knew he had left the hospital, she made an unfortunate decision: She told them that the boy had escaped and was okay.

Questions poured onto her. How did she know? Who told her? Such vagueness suggested a lack of trustworthiness of her news.

"Where could he have gone? Is he in a safe place?" Sofia asked in a trembling voice.

A few days passed. Finally, Laura couldn't contain herself and called Sofia aside. "I hold all of you in confidence, but there are things that shouldn't be said except at the right time. It could do harm. But I will tell you, if you can keep it secret."

"What? And why me?"

"Do you promise to keep it secret?" Laura pressed.

Sofia hesitated. She found it strange, but almost guessing what it might be, said, "I promise."

"Then be reassured, daughter. Miguel is in my house. He's well and he's safe."

A new torrent of questions rolled out. What kind of mood was he in? How did he spend his time? Had he spoken of her?

Laura answered everything with understanding, and with a bit of bad conscience. She knew there were things one needed to keep to oneself. Revealing to Sofia that Miguel was living in her house, she thought, went against that principle. And if, like herself, others also believed they could justify breaking their silence, it would end up destroying the whole security protocol.

That's what happened at the Pereira house. It wasn't long before everyone knew the secret. Everyone trustworthy, of course, so no harm came of it.

Life regained a certain calm at the Pereiras'. Visitors started reappearing regularly. But Sofia was not satisfied. She asked, "Couldn't I go to your house?"

"Don't push it, daughter," Laura answered. "Your house could still be under surveillance." It was well-known that Laura went there. She never stopped doing so, and no one paid attention. But if Sofia crossed the street to Laura's house, that would provoke curiosity and questions. What was she doing there? And it would lead to more questions. Was someone else living there? Who? And doing what, if no one had been allowed to see them even once?

9

At last the reason why José Pedro stayed outdoors all those misty nights became clear: He was seeing if the Pereira house was being watched. He concluded it wasn't, and shared his observation with António, who said, "Let's wait a few more days. If there are no new developments, then he can come."

His stay with Laura had become difficult, almost unbearable. Laura would have wanted to keep him there with her. But Miguel was becoming more and more anxious, and it was only a matter of time before one of the neighbors would discover someone hiding in the house.

So a decision was made. José Pedro reinforced his vigilance, and if he saw nothing more, Miguel would move to the Pereira house. He needed only to casually cross the street and without a second to spare, the door would open and he would enter the Pereira house. And that's what they did.

He was received with joyous emotion. Sofia ran to him and kissed his face, where the pinkish scars from his lesions were still visible. Conceição and Ester kissed him, too. António and José Pedro slapped him robustly on his back.

In the large kitchen area, everyone surrounded him enthusiastically. "Sit down, have a seat," they repeated almost as a chorus.

Without hesitation, Sofia sat by his side, and the rest all around him. Endless questions, and ready responses.

Miguel began by telling of his escape from the hospital and what happened with the police: the beatings and tortures which the PIDE men sneeringly called small demonstrations of their product.

"At least they spoke the truth about that," António broke in, with unexpected zeal. "What they did to you was inhuman torture, but only demonstrations. You were brutally beaten for one or two hours. But there have been prisoners beaten all night long, even to death. They didn't let you sleep for two nights. But others they subjected to sleep torture for a whole week and even more. You were up against the wall for a couple of hours, but others whole days and nights until they were pissing blood. They put out a cigarette on the back of your hand, but some prisoners were left with their whole chest and arms studded with burns."

How did António know all that? To Miguel that was a surprising revelation, but to the rest of the people there it seemed quite ordinary. Why?

"Let's leave that for now," Conceição cut him off. "Tell us how you feel. I'll make coffee."

They drank coffee and remained talking far into the night. They gave him the grandmother's room to sleep in, as if affirming life and the future, superseding death and the past.

Family life went on, with its usual rhythms and the regular visitors.

To the closest neighbors, the only news was finding out that Miguel was hiding out there now as a fugitive from the police, and that the courtship between him and Sofia was practically official, recognized and respected by the family. In front of everyone, the lovers kissed when the girl went off to school and when she returned. At night, many times, the two of them tried to be by themselves, and when they were with others they behaved as if there were no one else there.

What they said to one another was nothing unusual. They spoke of current events and exchanged popular expressions of love.

"I love you so much," Sofia said, "that whatever happens, I never want it to separate us."

He laughed. He thought and felt the same. And one day, overcoming his timidity, he declared himself. "I want you to be my companion going forward in life. Okay?"

Their happiness over this prospect was overshadowed by the questions they asked themselves. Live together? How? When? Where? What would they do?

Miguel's talks with António, and sometimes also with José Pedro, became evermore open in the search for answers, and at the same time more uncertain about finding them. Still, matters evolved apace.

Talking once again about the PIDE torture, António asked a surprising question. "Were you afraid?"

Miguel didn't know what to respond to such a query out of the blue. Actually, he hadn't ever thought about it, and his response came out with extreme difficulty. Images of what he had suffered occurred to him as if out of a whirlwind. When he left the hospital and they brought him to the PIDE, above all he felt the failure of the escape. Then he recalled the physical pain and suffering, the pointless desire that it would stop, his denunciation of brutal torture and, shamefully, the scream he let out when they burned his hand with the cigarette. But except for that moment, never a complaint, never a shout, never begging them to stop the torture, or even being tempted to.

And now, surprised at himself, taking stock of his own comportment, he answered plainly, simply and truthfully, "I think I wasn't, I wasn't afraid."

"You are a brave one, Miguel," António commented. "It's good that you are aware of this and that you have confidence in yourself."

"It also good that your confidence not go to your head," José Pedro added, "and that you demonstrate it in everything you do in life."

Another time, António advanced a question that made his friend shudder. "What do you think you'll do? Spend your whole life hidden here?"

Up to that point he hadn't thought about it. For the first time ever, he felt at home in this house. He felt himself loved and cared for under the same roof as Sofia, and being comfortable with her. And strangely, just as in the hospital, obsessed with Cláudia, he had forgotten Sofia, now it seems that out of his love for Sofia, he had forgotten Cláudia.

It would be absurd to say yes, he wanted to stay there forever. But go where? And do what? Leave Sofia?

Although he understood the young man's chagrin, António repeated his question. "Are you thinking of living your whole life hidden here?"

Miguel answered unavoidably, "No, naturally not," but in a grumbling, almost offended tone.

Sensing that Miguel might have misunderstood his words, António took another tack. "You're right, Miguel. But you're aware, of course, that you just responded to the question, without thought about a solution to the situation." After a short pause, he continued calmly and tenderly, "We all like having you with us, and we appreciate you a lot, Miguel, as if you were one of the family. You and Sofia love one another and we don't want to stand in your way."

Miguel let out an expression of relief. But António continued, "What we need is to resolve all this. We have to find a solution."

"But what?" Miguel excitedly interrupted.

"We'll think it over, but we'll find one."

In later conversation, António prodded Miguel to deeper reflection. "You endured a brutal attack; you were tortured by the PIDE. Surely you must have thought it had something to do with the situation in Portugal, and it would be good to change it."

He understood. But he did not see how to change it.

António seemed satisfied with that answer. And what he said then was decisive for the young man's grasp of consciousness. "Changing the situation will not happen by itself. Only the people's struggle will make it possible."

Drawn into these ideas, Miguel asked himself, *Struggle? How? With whom?*

António anticipated such doubts. "A lot of people are struggling, and I will tell you who. Do you recall when they said to you at the PIDE that what was a sample for you was nothing compared to what they did to others? Did they ever say who these others were?"

A phrase soared to Miguel's memory that he heard when they were beating him: *Take that, you fucking Commie!* He, a "Commie?" He, a Communist? Ridiculous. But the phrase revealed who were the victims, at least the main victims, of torture and assassination.

"The Communists are the main fighters," said António, as if he were pronouncing the most commonplace statement.

"But I'm not a Communist—"

António laughed, "—but you could become one."

As their conversations ensued, Miguel felt himself transported to a different world, one he never knew existed. The words were different, the ideas, the emotions, and the revelation of the kind of society they lived in and how to confront it.

The revelation deepened day by day, especially when António and he talked alone together. Farther along, António returned to an earlier theme: "I once told you that the best and most courageous fighters against the dictatorship, against the PIDE and its crimes, and for a transformation of our situation, are the Communists, and that you could become one." And, chuckling in semi-seriousness, he added, "It seems to me you almost are one without knowing it."

"Me?!"

"Yes, you."

Some days later he made his intention clearer with a concrete proposal. "If you've made up your mind, I can connect you with the Party and you can get out of Lisbon to a safe location."

Miguel interrupted him, "And Sofia?"

"Sofia will go with you, naturally. It's what she wants."

Days later he spoke even more precisely. "For some years you will have to learn how to hide yourselves and avoid being followed. You can be what we call a support point, a safe house. You'll receive a salary, modest but enough." And laughing, he added, "Watch out! You had such trouble staying hidden at Laura's house. Now that you'll really have to learn to hide yourself, let's see if you become impatient with that."

"There won't be any problem," Miguel said quietly.

These same ideas and prospects came up between the two lovers. "Father told me we two could live together in a clandestine house outside of Lisbon, and asked if I felt all right about going with you. And I told him yes."

These words spoken, they drew together, embraced and kissed. Their kiss was different now from any before, a kiss of intense desire, breaking through barriers and resistance, a desire to possess with urgency and need.

The next day, Sofia spoke. "You know me well. I will be your companion in life. Do you remember I told you I had a secret that I would reveal at the right time? That time has come. I don't know, because I never told you before, if you'll continue to love me in the same way."

She recounted how at school, aside from her studies, she belonged to the leadership of the student association, which struggled for better conditions for students, for open access to the library, for a lunchroom where you could get modest meals at a reasonable cost, and for a sports field.

"And can you guess why I did all that?"

"I think I guessed—"

And before Sofia could reveal her secret, he revealed it himself: "Because you're a Communist!"

"Correct, comrade," Sofia said, and they roared with laughter.

10

The decision was made: Miguel and Sofia would move to the outskirts of Lisbon, where Miguel would not be so easily recognized. It had been decided what they were going to do—to establish a safe house for clandestine work. Everyone launched into preparations for the trip.

Conceição, with António's consent, now took an initiative no one foresaw. She called Sofia and Miguel, and with emotion in her voice, said, "Children, you're going to live together—"

"Married," Sofia corrected, playfully.

"What's the point of going around hiding in the shadows?" And she led them into Miguel's room. The bed was made with a pretty folded sheet and a soft blanket freshly ironed. "From here on, this is your room."

The three of them embraced and kissed.

Everything seemed clear. But some things were not—nothing terrible with serious consequences, but real, unfortunate, and avoidable.

Sofia, for example, began right away, but secretly, buying things to take with them. And when she figured she had made all her purchases, she put them on display in the room like an exposition. Pots and other kitchen utensils, a coffeemaker, dishes, clothes for the house, night clothes, and her personal wardrobe, everything brand new. Also proudly displayed were half a dozen big cardboard boxes, a new suitcase and a basket.

Miguel helped her arrange the show, and they called the family in to see.

The immediate reactions threw the young couple off. António Pereira lovingly embraced his daughter. Ester had a good laugh and at the same time made a loving fuss over them. Conceição kissed both of them and started crying.

Once these first responses quieted down, the discussion turned more serious, while still loving. They couldn't take all those things; they'd have to settle down first; on the trip they should only take a small load, maybe the suitcase and maybe also the basket or a few bags of items.

"Everything else will stay here in safe keeping until it can be sent to you," Conceição promised.

Even dreams with modest objectives can be profoundly felt. Which explains why it was Sofia who cried the most. For several days she appeared inconsolable, and almost indifferent to her coming departure. Then, one morning, she woke up, confident and happy.

They spoke at the back of the house, in the large kitchen space. Everyone was there, and everyone could hear. But in the exchange of impressions about Sofia and Miguel and the specific tasks they would be taking on, only José Pedro and António intervened.

One by one the details were laid out: The best way to protect yourself, living a normal life, relations with your neighbors, security rules for coming and going at the house, the indispensable discipline.

Lia and José Pedro handled the departure: They entered the house by the trail on the garden side and hid the car that would transport the couple behind the shed for the garden tools.

Lia, António, José Pedro, Sofia and Miguel worked out many aspects of the trip and of the tasks. But there was still time for some light talk.

Watching Lia, now with blonde hair, Ester found the comrade's new look strange. In the past it seemed to her that her beautiful black hair attracted attention. Now, it seemed, her friend had dyed her hair blonde—worse still, if she intended it as a disguise. With her usual frankness, she said, "Listen, Lia. Don't you think dyeing your hair blonde only calls more attention to you?"

Lia answered with a touch of irony. "It's not my fault. It's the way I was born." And she smiled because, in fact, blonde was her natural hair color.

With Sofia she engaged in a different kind of conversation. "You're coming with us," Sofia asked, "and then we won't see you again?"

"I'm not deserting you there, but you must be patient with me. It won't be every day, but we'll see each other," Lia responded.

As Lia and José Pedro had arrived, so Lia, Sofia and Miguel left through the garden, carrying only the baggage allowed. José Pedro stayed with the Pereiras. It was a painful goodbye, but looked toward a future agreed to by all. Lia drove the car in the city.

Lia let them out of the car, and from that point the couple took a jitney, a clunky old vehicle that filled rapidly and left in a sputter that sounded like tin cans clanging. It started off in first gear, then accelerated into second rising up low slopes under a scalding sun. They choked on the smell of burning gas and oil on the inclines, giving way to a breeze of fresh air at the top of the hills. Then, on the descent, the vehicle coasted almost silently, only broken up by the chirruping of the motor.

With squinting eyes they could easily make out the undulating terrain of the outskirts of Lisbon.

After an hour or so in the jitney, it stopped in the market square of a larger town, where a veritable ant colony of people moved hurriedly to and fro.

Very soon, another jitney arrived. As a public transportation junction, the square came alive with a new throng of hundreds of scurrying people almost trampling over one another searching for their next ride—men, women, children, most of them middle-aged, a diverse crowd in a variety of dress. Everyone had the air about them of someone who knew where they were going and for what reason. One young girl, holding her shopping bags, stood above and apart from the others by her gentle, modest beauty.

Crossing the square with the group of passengers they had accompanied, Sofia noticed Miguel's unusual behavior. He was turning his head to one side and then the other, as if looking for something he wasn't sure he had seen.

"What's wrong?" she asked.

"Nothing, nothing."

He didn't give a definite answer and was never quite able to find it for himself, when later recalling the incident. The fact is that, in the crowd of all those people, he thought he saw Cláudia, loaded with shopping bags, and losing herself in the multitude.

After a few more steps, they picked up another jitney. Side by side, Miguel and Sofia sat with their arms laced the whole trip, holding one another silently. Every so often, observing her companion's sad and distracted expression, Sofia squeezed him a little closer. Miguel answered her gesture with a tender touch. The rest of the trip, they did not speak.

The Pereira family moved on with their customary life. As always, António left early for work with his calm attitude and assured pace, and returned at night with the same contentment and security. Ester went to her regular job. Conceição tended to the house. Saturdays and Sundays, they worked the vegetable and flower gardens, now without Sofia. The usual visitors kept coming—José Pedro, Laura, and Tó. Lia showed up from time to time, too. On the street, as ever, the Pereira family was considered a normal and exemplary family.

Except for two differences on the street: Sofia's absence and no one knowing anything about Miguel. After what happened between Miguel and his father, it was no wonder he didn't return. But people did ask about Sofia, and Laura explained. "She's a very bright girl, you know, and she got a scholarship for a course of study in France."

That news spread quickly, and no one was surprised. Generally, they believed, such a family, with all its fine points, deserved a lucky break like that.

And so the very well guarded mysteries were preserved.

The 3rd Floor

THE "3rd Floor" was the 3rd floor of a prison. Its entranceway had an iron grate and a metal-lined door.

Inside, an enormous hall with three grated windows on one side overlooked the street and, on the other, a doorway led into a long dining area from which, through one more window, one could look out onto an alley where the neighbors hung their clothes out to dry.

Off the dining room was a door to the washrooms and toilets.

During the day, with the folding beds raised up and leaning against the walls, the 3rd Floor was a large empty space where prisoners could circulate.

At night, at bedtime, the prisoners lowered the beds and stretched them out in two long rows, one next to the other, almost without space in between.

At the end of the Floor, beyond an open doorway, was the "Room." It had a single grated window matching the row of three windows in the main hall, a water closet, half a dozen small iron beds and a table.

In the Room, one prisoner ate standard prison grub. The others received their meals from the outside, which was the case on the Floor only with Karl, a Jewish German aviator imprisoned there.

Such a huge difference between the 3ʳᵈ Floor and the Room provoked comment and mordant jokes. "This side is for us, the proletarians. The Room is for the bourgeoisie," Valdo proclaimed with a laugh.

Some from the Room left at times for the Floor just to stretch their legs. No one there knew why they had been put in prison. They didn't speak to anyone and returned to the Room without saying a word. Had they given their comrades away under interrogation?

One exception was Rudolfo. He left the Room frequently, as though he needed to breathe more air. Merry and playful, he fit in with one and all and ate the pitiful food with them.

Up to that point no one had seen Chagas leave the Room. Well known as a spy, he maintained suspect relations with other prisoners, whom the International Police for the Defense of the State—the PIDE—had sent to be near him.

It being summer, almost everyone walked about in shirt-sleeves or undershirts, with only three exceptions. Rudolfo did not give up his beautiful pullover. And two Polish officers who had fled from the war, wore suits and ties all day long. Only at night did they take them off to curl themselves up under the sheets; but first thing in the morning, when they got up, after a brief trip to the bathroom, they took care to tie the knots in their ties, comb their hair and put on their jackets.

Party members António, Filipe and Vítor commanded deep respect on the Floor. They had a style of leadership all their own, with their soft, persuasive voices never attempting to pressure a decision. Nevertheless, their opinions were taken as directives for the Communist prisoners—which most of the prisoners there were—and accepted by the others.

Such was the situation on the 3ʳᵈ Floor during the first years of the Second World War.

2

The dawn bell sounded. The prisoners got up, set their beds back up against the wall, and rushed to the washrooms and toilets. They dressed quickly.

Shortly after, the grated gate and the reinforced entrance door opened with the sharp metallic clanging of the bolts. Then the prison aides entered with two enormous coffee urns and a bag of bread crusts, and brought it all to the dining hall.

With mugs in hand, the prisoners queued up. They were tired of complaining. The "coffee" was an obscure watery solution, and the crusts all but inedible.

"The crumbs are only good for plugging up holes in the wall," said Beja solemnly one day, he of the white beard, esteemed by all as a solid defender of traditional values from the 1910 Republic that the fascists overthrew in 1926.

The prisoners accepted the meal, one might say, with unexpected resignation and patience. The fact is that, after the last fight for better conditions, many had been transferred out to other prisons, such as Peniche and Caxias, and new inmates had come to take their places who were not yet integrated into the collectivity. The conditions were far from ripe for a strong protest, which would only have been met by inevitably violent repression.

So they imbibed their watery brown drink, took a nibble or two on the crust, went to the sinks to wash their mugs, and started cleaning. Brigades on a weekly schedule, with brooms, dustpans, pails and mops in their hands, all took part.

The cleaning finished, an interminable day lay before them. Groups of comrades ambled from one side to the other along the whole length of the Floor, some conversing and pausing from time to time, while some others inexplicably ran here and there as if rushing somewhere. In the dining hall, others read and wrote.

At one of the grated windows, Inácio, a young Communist, and Serafim, an old republican, fed breadcrumbs to the pigeons, which flocked in with the sweet rustle of their beating wings. Hovering midair, they snared little morsels of bread with their beaks and hurried away, making room for the others. Coming and going occupied the whole morning.

"Where do all those pigeons come from?" young Inácio asked. "I'd like to know."

"Not difficult," old Serafim answered. "Either they come from the Rossio, or the Carmo ruins, or from Terreiro do Paço."

"Very well," Inácio smiled. "Or from the Cais do Sodré, or Largo Camões, or São Pedro de Alcântara," he said. "It's not difficult to know."

Serafim patted him on his back, friendly and with gentle irony. "You got it right, my friend. As you can see, it's not difficult."

3

A few days later, just after the cleaning, the bolts on the grate and the plated door resounded. Two guards appeared and scanned the room. Someone was coming.

Before long, the guards stepped aside and noisily shut the door and the gate. A prisoner entered the Floor, an unexpected figure, his beard grown out, head shaved, his pants tattered, his worn-down shoes creating an unstable gait. His face was stained with black blotches. He had a mug in his hand.

Karl drew closer to see, and right away, disdainfully stepped back.

Valdo approached the new arrival, curious. "Look at this. Now they're arresting wretches like him," he sighed.

Wretches? Valdo was mistaken. The newcomer took a couple of steps in, to everyone's surprise. And suddenly, a shocking exclamation rang out: "You? Augusto? What happened?"

Filipe recognized him and ran to embrace him. Everyone turned around and led him straight to the dining hall not knowing what to do.

Rudolfo left the Room, looked around, saw the situation, went back into the Room and came out again with clothes and slippers in his hands. "Excuse me, Filipe. You'll have time to talk later, but we have to take care of him now."

He handed the clothes to Augusto. "Wash up, get dressed, put these slippers on, and then let us know if you want your beard cut."

"Don't cut it," young Inácio broke in, "it looks good on him."

"If he wants his beard cut, I'll do it," Beja of the white beard joined in.

Before he went back in, Rudolfo turned to Filipe, half seriously, half in jest. "Here on the Floor someone said we're the bourgeois in the Room. So you see, there are bourgeois who are useful for something."

After a little while, Augusto reappeared. He still had his beard, but all cleaned up and with new clothes he looked transformed.

"Did you eat already?" they asked.

"Yes, I ate."

The comrades stepped aside so Filipe and the newcomer could continue talking.

Filipe had worked in the factory with him and both had belonged to the Party cell there. But it had been years since they'd seen one another, and Filipe had no idea what assignments the comrade had undertaken since then.

Briefly, Augusto recounted how he'd been tortured for three months incommunicado. The PIDE wanted him to disclose the whereabouts of the leading comrade for whom he and someone else, named Garcia, had secured the house of a family that gave him cover when he came to Lisbon. The house was raided, the comrade managed to escape, the family was brought in to the PIDE, and he and Garcia arrested.

"The worst part is that Garcia, like me, knows where the comrade is."

Augusto did not talk. But he was worried about Garcia. When they took him out of isolation, Augusto crossed paths with him for a couple of minutes at PIDE, and Garcia told him something that he couldn't forget: "I don't know if I can hold out."

Augusto didn't know where they had taken him and feared he might have caved.

"Here," Filipe told him, "we have contact with the Party outside. We'll try to warn the comrades in time. We'll see if we can take care of this tomorrow."

At lunch, Valdo, without the guard overhearing, asked one of the aides, "Listen, partner, why did they shave our comrade's head?"

"Lice," the aide answered, catching himself by surprise for having responded.

"Fantastic!" Valdo laughed. "They say they shaved his head because of lice. And left the beard for the lice to go out to pasture!"

"It was just to humiliate him, nothing more," Inácio observed.

4

The visiting room was a vast space divided down the middle by a double set of metal screens the whole length across.

On one side sat the prisoners, on the other the visitors. Between the two screens, a guard kept watch. It was an efficient system, where everything could be heard. Neither prisoners nor visitors could touch, nor pass anything back and forth between them.

That day António, Filipe, Augusto and Valdo had visitors. Also Raul and Belmiro, recently arrested for painting graffiti at night, and Karl, the German Jew.

Their visitors were all relatives, except Karl's. The man who visited him was well dressed and good-looking, Portuguese for sure, because he could be heard speaking to a guard, but he spoke with Karl in German.

The conversations, listened to attentively, ranged around currents events. Questions from relatives, general information about the prisoners, questions from the prisoners, all touching on everyday matters. So as not to raise any suspicion from the guards, some questions nonetheless were imbedded with ciphered language.

Leaning against the grated divider, Augusto's wife couldn't stop crying seeing her husband like that. Although clean shaven now, and with fresh clothes, he was barely recognizable with his shaved head and the marks of torture plainly visible on his face.

"What have you heard about my brother?" was one of her husband's many questions.

His wife understood that he was referring to Garcia.

"Nothing," she replied, alarmingly.

António had a visit from his wife Mariana and their ten-year-old son, who had been born just a few days before he was taken prisoner. No one could find it strange that he asked his son, "Hey, Francisco, how long has it been since you've had a haircut?"

That question, however, had a far greater significance because it was in fact directed at Mariana, and meant: "In the shirt I'm giving you to wash, you'll find an urgent message for the Party."

Clothes turned over for washing, clothes returned clean. Message sent, message received.

Returning to the 3rd Floor, António did not seek out his comrades. He put on his freshly cleaned shirt, went to be alone in the water closet, and there retrieved the message in the shirt his wife had brought.

That same afternoon, still extremely agitated coming off the visit, and almost guessing what the comrades might be trying to undertake with the Party, Augusto cornered Filipe. "Listen, Filipe. I just arrived here a short time ago, but looking at these windows and doors, a question has entered my mind. Wouldn't it be possible for us to escape from here?"

Augusto warranted confidence. But Filipe understood that he should not tell him what the three Party leaders were planning with the Party outside.

"That's a question we should all be thinking about," he replied.

The next day, António informed Filipe and Vítor about the message received. As usual, with caution not to be overheard, they walked back and forth from side to side on the Floor.

The three comrades knew how the message was hidden—written by António in pencil on a single sheet of cigarette paper, in letters so small they were next to impossible to read. The paper was meticulously folded into eighths, well placed in the placket panel next to a button. Even the writer would have had a hard time finding this minuscule hidden paper, so perfectly concealed as it was.

On the outside, the comrades did the same thing writing to the prisoner.

The main theme of the message received: In response to the question previously posed, the Party states that the grated windows on the 3rd Floor face the street.

Theme of the next outgoing message: Asking the Party to verify and inform if on the street, under the windows, there are night guards with or without sentry box. The message also reported Augusto's arrival, the tortures he endured for three months, his valiant comportment, and his doubts concerning Garcia's behavior.

"António, it's extraordinary how you can possibly write all that on a cigarette paper," Vítor commented.

"Good eyesight and experience," he responded.

The fact that on the Floor the most serious things generally were under control did not mean that from time to time there was no discord.

That happened with a little incident that took place at twilight that same day.

Next to a window, a group was listening to Valdo's jokes. "President Carmona went to a town. There was a solemn meeting and Carmona was discoursing. 'Ladies and gentlemen. This is the second time I've come to your area. You will understand, however, this is not the first time. That's why this is the second time so you'll be sure to understand—'"

Rudolfo, who had stepped out of the Room, had already reached the group standing under the grated window. Valdo interrupted his tale, remembering what he had said about Rudolfo just days before. "That's all for now. We now have the bourgeoisie listening to stories."

Rudolfo did not appreciate that and turned aggressive. "Listen here, kid, be careful what you say." And he advanced toward the youth in a foul mood.

Valdo was about to say something, but his companions led him away.

"If you continue like that, one of these days you're going to get burned," Inácio told him.

5

As it grew dark outside, they brought in three men from Alentejo, south of Lisbon. Looking the other prisoners over but not recognizing anyone, they acted with reserve. Their reason for imprisonment was all they said about themselves. In their border town, they had lent support and protection to a group of Spaniards fleeing from the August 14, 1936, massacre at Badajoz.

"So you were arrested? And the Spaniards?"

"They were apprehended and then handed over to Franco's troops at the border. Certainly to be shot."

They had been in the hands of the PIDE for only a week before being sent to the 3rd Floor. What the PIDE was interested in, they already knew. They only left them with one piece of advice: "Don't tell anyone about this, otherwise you'll come back here and we'll make it even uglier for you."

They seemed unconcerned, as though going to prison was of no great importance. Only at the evening meal, things started to sour, with the conger stew. They started to eat, and immediately spat out the tiny bones.

"Listen, comrades," someone counseled. "Do like us. Take the fish out and eat the potatoes. They're the tail ends, and no one can eat them."

"A lamb stew would be nicer, no?" No one responded to the joke, and the conversation stopped there.

The next morning, they drank the coffee water without objection, but left the bread crusts on the table. The guard asked who left them, and they said they didn't want to eat them.

"Keep the bread," the guard ordered. They shrugged their shoulders and kept the bread.

They were told to help out with the cleaning and they did so, not well, but obligingly. One of them said to another, "Ay, Zé, what would our wives say to us if they saw us like this...."

The cleaning done, the sound level died down. Suddenly, two voices in harmony rang out, in the deep, resonant singing of Alentejo. And to the general wonderment, another prisoner, also an Alentejano, who had been on the 3rd Floor for a long time without anyone knowing where he was from, cut through the strong chant of his two countrymen with his fine, evocative high tenor.

The enchanted audience applauded.

But already the sound of clanging bolts banged, the gate and the metal-plated door opened and two guards broke in threateningly and shouted, "Silence! What's happening here?"

The singers had two more verses: "Alentejo land of mine / Fragrant of carnation and rosemary." And only then did they stop, remaining calmly standing.[1]

The guards withdrew, and everyone was waiting for what would happen. But to everyone's surprise, nothing did.

6

The lunch of black-eyed peas with albacore and minced onion led to conflict. The aides had placed an enormous pot on the dining hall table and served rations of it onto aluminum plates that the prisoners in line held out before sitting down.

Mona entered to supervise the meal. This guard loved to instigate and create excuses to impose punishment.

Inácio and Valdo seated themselves beside Túlio, a young man who had been suffering a fever with no attention from the authorities. Daytime, he remained lying on the floor. The day before, they had lowered his bed, but a guard came and ordered it lifted again.

He sat at the table with Valdo's assistance.

"You there! What are you waiting for?" Mona shouted at Túlio. Half dead, he didn't respond.

"Sir, don't you see he's sick?" Valdo intervened.

"And you?" Mona accused. "Who told you to speak? It's him who should answer."

Valdo insisted, "It's my duty to help my comrade."

"And it's my duty to know what mine is," Mona shot back.

Valdo would not be contained. "It appears you do not know!"

"When lunch is over, you'll see if I know or not," Mona growled.

Everyone felt that any reaction from the others would provoke a repression of unforeseeable fury, and they were not prepared to resist it. But Raul and Belmiro did not see it that way.

"You don't have the right to punish our comrade," Raul spoke out.

---

1. A short video on Cante Alentejano can be viewed here: https://www.youtube.com/watch?v=OGmCNJ6RGEs.

"Fascist!" Belmiro exclaimed in a loud voice.

"If that's what you want, that's what you'll get," said Mona with disarming calm. "It was only one of you, now it's three."

The aides removed the pot, and Mona left with them.

The comrades helped Túlio to stretch out on the floor, wrapping him in a blanket. The others surrounded Valdo, Belmiro and Raul. Everyone feared what might come, but at the same time reveled in the sweet resistance.

It didn't last long. The gate rumbled, the bolt snapped the plated door open, and Mona spat out, "Valdo, Belmiro and Raul, to the head office!"

On leaving, Valdo turned his head back. "Amuse yourselves, comrades!" he quipped with a cheery air.

The other two waved goodbye.

They didn't come back that day, nor in the following days.

António, Filipe and Vítor debated if the stance they took was correct or not, not to intervene in the incident. Did the fact that they were engaged in an escape plan justify not putting themselves forward in this contest so as to avoid being transferred? They themselves had their doubts. They decided that the escape plan constituted the first priority for their conduct, but also considered what they might do to try to resolve Túlio's situation.

António, sentenced many years before as a leader of the Party, commanded a certain respect among his jailers. He asked for a meeting with the prison director, but it was the head guard who received him.

"If you do not address the situation of my comrade Túlio," António said, "what is happening here will end up becoming known."

"I have no fear of that," the head guard limited himself to saying. And he sent him back to the Floor.

A new cigarette paper in tiny print exposed the case in another patient labor of hiding it in the placket of a shirt sent out to wash.

One week later, António was called again to the head guard's office. "Read this. It had to be you that informed." And he showed him a little leaflet on silk paper: "Save Túlio Martins!"

"He's going to the infirmary," said the head guard, "but don't think it's because of this little piece of paper. It's something we had already decided."

"Perfect," was António's only comment.

That same day, a guard appeared with a prison nurse in a white smock. They took Túlio to the infirmary on the sixth floor.

A week later, they brought Raul and Belmiro back to the 3rd Floor. They had been beaten and placed in isolation in the dungeon. Nothing was known of Valdo.

7

This problem was thus resolved, but the prison director and the head guard were furious, which explains what happened as a result.

António was in the dining hall writing a letter to his family, when the head guard entered, with Mona alongside. He went directly to him.

"Why are you writing with invisible ink?" he asked aggressively, pointing to the letter António was writing.

"No, chief. Just blue ink," he answered.

"We'll see about that," the head guard replied. And ripping the letter out of António's hands, he lit a lighter and brought it close to the paper to warm it. The PIDE obviously had taught them that, writing between the lines with urine, nothing could be seen when it dried, but once heated, what was written would appear.

But he had learned that lesson poorly. He brought the letter too close to the lighter and it caught fire. He left immediately, fleeing the fiasco, but added, "Remember, you cannot fool me. And we'll see further about this correspondence business."

The next day, several were called to the head office. On top of the table sat a mountain of letters received and never delivered to the prisoners, and another of letters from the prisoners never placed in the mail.

They all heard the same speech. That correspondence was only authorized to a wife and children, and prisoners could only write and receive one letter per month. Always subject to censorship, of course.

What happened with Beja became the subject of much laughter on the 3rd Floor. The head guard had in his hands a letter that Beja had asked to be mailed.

"Look here! Who is this Dolfo about whom you're asking for news? We don't have any record that you have a son by that name."

"It's not my son, it's my dog."

"Your dog? Whatever. Anyway, the letter is not being sent."

They told António to sit at a table. In front of him they placed a sheet of paper, a pen and a small receptacle with some unknown liquid. "Go ahead, wet the point and write whatever you want."

Antonio wrote: "Invisible ink."

They waited a good ten minutes and then heated the paper with an iron. Almost certainly, the liquid was urine and the words "invisible ink" became visible, though hard to read.

"So?" the head guard exclaimed triumphantly.

"Excuse me, chief, the pen point made an impression on the paper and the letters are unclear. I should have written with a toothpick."

"But in the end, do you or do you not know about sympathetic inks, or invisible ink, as you call it? Was I right or wrong?"

"Naturally I know about them, and many others as well. I simply do not use them in my correspondence."

António related the story to Filipe and Vítor. "You gave them good answers," Vítor said. "But this incident shows us the necessity to redouble your caution when you write messages to the Party."

"I will take greater care. And if it's necessary, the remedy will be chewing them up and swallowing them," Augusto laughed.

8

By trading with their companions, António, Filipe and Vítor had arranged to occupy the three beds in a row closest to the last grated window on the Floor. Escaping from the prison and returning to the struggle was their daylong preoccupation.

They saw only one way out: Saw through the window bars and lower themselves to the street by a rope of torn sheets. But to succeed, they would have to solve a series of problems.

They had already received word from the Party that there was a guardhouse at street level under the window, where a night guard served duty. How to overcome this challenge? Could the comrades on the outside muffle the guard at precisely the time when, with the bars sawn, they would descend to the street? It wouldn't be easy.

In any case, if they were thinking of sawing the bars, they would need a special saw. Filipe and Vítor posed the question: How to get one?

António cut them off. "Leave that to me." And he repeated it, as if the problem were already solved. "Leave that to me."

With that, the discussion was closed for the day.

That afternoon, at visiting time, Augusto got bad news. His wife, evermore anxious, told him through coded language that nothing was known of Garcia.

"I don't like this," Augusto told Filipe. "Either he's talking, or PIDE is still working on him to talk."

There was nothing to be done. They had to wait.

9

No one ever figured out who Karl the German was. An aviator, as he said? A Jew, as he claimed? The government imprisoned both civilians and military who had fled from the war, most of them strange and dubious cases. Karl wasn't the only strange case; there were also the two Poles on the 3rd Floor. But Karl was indeed a mystery.

He had his visitor, an important person in government or police spheres, which was obvious from the way he addressed the prison guards and from the obsequious manner in which they listened to him.

The German's comportment raised a number of questions. If he was Jewish, how could he have been a German aviation officer? If he enjoyed such high protection, why was he there? Why did they keep him on the 3rd Floor and not in the Room? Why, if he was on the Floor, did he receive his meals from the outside? Why did he adopt that way of isolating himself from the other prisoners, observing what happened, but always remaining silent and removed from what was going on?

His day arrived. He was called to the head office. Upon his return, he grabbed the suitcase that he had stored in the locker above his bed, and when they came for him, he left without a word or gesture of goodbye to anyone.

That same day they brought Valdo back to the Floor. He entered in a good mood, as though nothing had happened. And, in full view of questioning eyes, he went straight to Filipe, spoke with him and then made the rounds of the Floor talking with the others.

He reported that he had spent the week in secret isolation, a small cell without even a peephole or hatch, a metal-plated door and a cement floor with no mattress, only a blanket.

"It must have been hard passing the time," Filipe observed.

"Oh, there was much to do. Killing bedbugs is a lot of work."

10

They brought a new prisoner up to the 3rd Floor, just like Augusto, in a horrible state—hair razored off, beard grown out, eyes all black and blue, face badly beaten, upper lip split and bloody. The guards showed him an unoccupied bed and left.

António, Filipe and Vítor sat with him at the dining table. In a few words, he said he was a Party functionary responsible for transporting the Party paper *Avante!* to various regions. Having been seized in the street, he didn't understand how they had found him, nor how they knew he was carrying the papers. The PIDE tried to force him into saying where he lived, where he picked up the papers, who gave them to him and to whom he delivered them. He was brutally beaten, but said nothing.

"What's your name, comrade?"

"Alberto's my real name, Rocha my Party name."

Coming out of the Room, Rudolfo once again offered his aid—scissors, shaving cream, razor blade, clean clothes.

Passing by Valdo, in a mock angry tone he said, "As you see, young man, the bourgeois still have some purpose."

"Bravo," Valdo replied.

With his visible signs of torture, Alberto showed himself to be strong and decisive. When the meeting with the three comrades ended, he asked a question—the same one Augusto had asked. "Comrades, wouldn't it be possible to escape from here?"

"Good question," António answered. "Today, get some rest. You need it. We'll talk about that as soon as we can."

As soon as he arrived, just like Augusto, Alberto posed the crucial question, which went straight to the core of the others' concerns and plans for escape.

The news sent by the Party, however, was not encouraging. Now they issued another warning. If the comrades were planning to escape out the window, lowering themselves to the street, they had to be aware of a problem.

Below the 3ʳᵈ floor, where they were held, a stone ledge ran all across the façade of the building. That was clearly the former top of the building, because many years ago they had remodeled and added two more stories.

"It's a good thing they told us. So now we know. When we jump, we first have to set foot on that ledge."

"If we hadn't known, we'd have fallen for sure," Vítor observed.

The three comrades collectively examined every issue concerning the escape. They had to invent solutions in the absence of experience. Vítor, especially, hardly thought of anything else.

He deliberated on every detail. How, when and where, without the Floor seeing, would they cut the sheets to improvise the rope they'd use to descend? How much time would the descent take in order to coincide with the help they'd get outside? How to cover up their progress on the sawing? What was the schedule of the prison guards' night rounds?

When the three discussed these problems, it was generally Vítor who proposed the ways of solving them.

11

The food had become intolerable. At lunch they insisted on serving albacore exuding the nauseating smell of spoiled fish and rancid oil. Four comrades—Valdo, Inácio, Belmiro and Raul—approached António.

"It can't go on like this," they said. "If we don't protest the food, either they're going to poison us with rotten fish, or they'll kill us from hunger."

One thought immediately struck António: *If the repression against a food uprising led to wholesale transfers out of the prison, that was the end of the escape plan.*

He and the other Party leaders on the 3rd Floor supported the food rebellion and would participate in it, but would not assume its direction.

"I understand," Valdo said, perhaps guessing the reason for such reservation. "We're not asking you to lead or direct the struggle. We will lead it. We just want to be sure you will support it and participate."

At lunch time, the aides brought the albacore in again. Mona, on guard, saw right away that everyone remained seated, and no one asked to be served.

Hand on his billy-club, he went to Valdo, who rose from the table. "So? You're not eating?"

"Guard, sir," Valdo began with a certain solemnity, "tell the director of the prison—"

"I am the director here, understand?" Mona shouted. "You're going to eat, like it or not." He advanced toward Valdo. "Are you eating or not?"

"Eat it yourself!" Valdo parried back.

In one bound, Inácio, Belmiro and Raul all rose, too, and the general revolt was launched. Everyone shouted their reasons for the food uprising.

For the first time in months, Chagas came out of the Room to observe.

The bolts on the gate and the plated door sounded. Four more guards burst in, protecting the exit. The aides removed the pots, amidst whoops and jeers.

Mona had completely lost control of the situation. As he exited, he turned around to speak: "You guys have no idea what's going to be done with you!"

Valdo still had time to throw back, "Tell the director of the prison that if the food continues like this, we'll make a hunger strike!"

The gate and the door closed with a clamor, the bolts locked, and a round of applause broke out on the 3rd Floor.

The food rebellion had succeeded. Everyone had their opinion and exchanged impressions. Now they had to wait for the result—and the punishment.

The retaliation came first. The gate and the plated door opened, and six guards entered with billy-clubs in their fists. They called out, "Osvaldo de Sousa, João Belmiro, Raul Ribeiro, João Serafim. Gather your things to leave."

Silence on the 3ʳᵈ Floor. The comrades named removed their things from their lockers and circled the Floor. They were embraced by António, by Filipe, by Vítor. They embraced others, and said their goodbyes to all. At the exit, the guards shoved them forcefully against one another.

The question remained: Who had pointed out that group as the leaders of the food rebellion?

"It was Chagas who saw them when he came out of the Room to witness the scene," António allowed.

"If it was Chagas, he didn't see very well," observed Filipe. "They didn't call Inácio, who was part of the group. And they took Serafim, who wasn't."

Although he had not been called, Inácio retrieved his things from his locker and left with the others without the guards noticing the error. Only several minutes later did they come back and throw him violently back onto the Floor.

The four who were named did not return. Much later it was learned that, after being beaten, they had been transferred to Peniche Fortress.

12

Túlio returned to the 3ʳᵈ Floor in a good frame of mind. He was happy to be back with his comrades again, and seemed like a new man. He had spent two weeks in the infirmary, his high fever had passed, and he had regained his strength. He had a curious story to relate.

He met someone there no more and no less than a big Dutch banker.

"A banker?" The comrades couldn't believe it.

"Yes, the owner of a bank. A millionaire."

"Amazing!"

"Now we're getting the big bourgeoisie," Rudolfo laughed.

Túlio recounted that, according to what the banker himself said, he was Jewish and had fled before the advancing Nazi armies. With his family, lovers, and numerous retinue, they left from Rotterdam on a luxury yacht and docked in Lisbon. All those people wound up getting sent to a floor at the Caxias Fortress with a very classy arrangement. Food, music, parties, dancing—"a five-star hotel," said the prisoners at the fortress. As he said to Túlio, in his escape he had spent and lost half of his immense fortune. They had sent the banker to the 3rd Floor infirmary only because he had taken seriously ill.

Many of his listeners were curious to find out how Túlio got along with this man, the two of them isolated together in the infirmary's only room. A large group gathered around to hear.

Surprising though it may sound, his relations with the banker were not difficult. They spoke in Portuguese—the banker's somewhat broken—with a few words in French. They talked on and on, and there were some funny moments.

At the infirmary, next to the room with the two narrow iron beds, there was a second little compartment which they called the "dining room," where the two sat to take their meals.

"And were the meals good?"

It wasn't albacore. It was soup, a decent plate of fish with potatoes, and a banana.

"So it went well?"

"Yes, it went well, because I took charge of it. That's what happened with the banana."

"With the banana?"

"Yes, the banana."

Everything they served had to be eaten in the dining room. But since they didn't give you anything else between noon and seven o'clock, Túlio would hide his banana and take it to the bedroom.

The banker saw, but didn't take his into the room. He ate his right away, at lunch.

Until one day, when he saw Túlio hiding his banana under his shirt, he said to him, "You can take *aussi* my banana."

Túlio never expected such generosity, and an amusing dialogue ensued.

"Thank you, senhor Vernstein, but it's not right for me to eat two bananas. I'm good with just one."

"You not understand. Banana not be for you. Banana be *pour moi*."

"Then why don't you take it?"

"Not be legal. You take, I pay."

"Pay for what?"

"You take banana for me *manger*. I be rich, I pay good. And when you leave here I arrange you *travail* in Congo."

"And what did you answer?" one of Túlio's audience asked.

"You eat it for lunch. It'll be good for your guts."

"What the hell, you could have asked for a high price. Would have been good for the Party!"

"Maybe. But it gave me such a pleasure to teach a millionaire that money doesn't resolve everything."

13

For various reasons, the anxiety only increased. Augusto's wife came to visit, crying uncontrollably. He didn't understand why and returned from the visit very disturbed.

"Stay calm, friend," António told him.

In the message shortly found in the freshly washed shirt, they learned the explanation for the wife's convulsive crying.

The message came, as usual, on the folded cigarette paper in the shirt placket. It contained news of Garcia. He had been taken to Peniche, where they continued interrogating him. It was now known that he had been summoned to get ready to be transferred.

"If they send him here, we'll soon see," said Filipe.

After only a few days the gate and the reinforced door opened, and Garcia entered, well dressed, clean shaven, suitcase in hand. A guard accompanied him in, and escorted him directly to the Room.

"Bad sign," Augusto murmured.

"Augusto is very nervous," António told Vítor. "Speak to him and calm him down. I'll see Filipe about the situation and afterward we'll talk."

The Room being at full capacity, they brought Rudolfo onto the Floor, assigning him an empty bed. He didn't seem bothered by it. He arranged his things in his locker, and joined a group that was conversing near one of the grated windows.

"Welcome," said one of the group.

"I'm where I belong," he replied, uncharacteristically serious and sober.

Meanwhile, to assess the situation, António and Filipe got together, walking the length of the hall from one side to the other and speaking low.

Garcia's transfer, and their having placed him in the Room, were indeed bad signs. Either he had informed to the PIDE, or they were trying to get him to talk to Chagas in the Room. Rudolfo's transfer from the Room to the Floor was also significant. For a long time he had been singled out for his relations with the comrades on the 3rd Floor. With his departure from the Room, Chagas remained as the clearest route, making friends with Garcia, toward obtaining information that PIDE had not yet been able to extract.

In the message hidden in António's clean shirt came responses to the latest questions: One piece of good news, and the other bad.

The bad: As for the sentinel on night guard under the grated windows, the comrades saw tremendous difficulty in addressing this. If the sentinel were overcome by force (only after which the fugitives could jump), an alarm would go off, and before they would reach the street level, the whole place would be swarming with guards.

In compensation, there was good news: The stone ledge led all the way to the roof of the neighboring building. "We have to closely examine this possibility," said António.

"Very hard to get there, very complicated," Filipe observed.

Wouldn't it be worth going back to the idea of escaping through the grated window in the dining hall?

"Unworkable," said Vítor. That had been the first consideration. But soon they concluded that getting up on the Floor in the middle of the night and going over to the dining hall window to saw the bars, they'd be in the direct view of their companions getting up to use the washrooms.

"Then let's study escaping on the stone ledge and the neighboring roof," António insisted.

14

Vítor came upon António in the empty washroom performing some weird exercise. Turned to the wall, pressing his whole body against it from head to toe, the open palms of his hands at shoulder level, he went creeping along in that position.

At first sight, Vítor thought his comrade might need some help. "What is it? Are you feeling ill?" he asked.

But he noticed that António just continued inching onward.

Surprised by his friend's voice, António turned around, smiling with satisfaction. "It's possible," he whispered.

"What are you talking about?" Vítor asked, not knowing what he was seeing.

They left the washroom to take a walk on the Floor, and António explained. He was trying to establish if it was or was not possible to glide the length of the building façade on the stone ledge whose existence the comrades had confirmed.

"Impossible!" Vítor asserted.

"Or not," António retorted.

Vítor shook his head no: "Impossible for me," he said. "If that's the decision, you guys can continue. But I can't join you. For a long time I've had vertigo in high places. We'd be kidding ourselves. I'd fall without a doubt. And you'd be dragged away with me."

He added, "If that's what you want to do, I'll help you every way I can: sawing the bars, covering up the cut, helping both of you in everything, whatever I can do."

He hesitated and said further, "Given that this is my problem, I don't want you to give up on this idea. But I have weighed it well. It seems to me too dangerous and risky. It's one thing to do an exercise here against the wall, but it's quite another, at the height of the 3ʳᵈ floor, with no support, to proceed along a stone ledge only the width of your foot."

António explained that, speaking for himself, it was just an experiment. They still needed to continue discussing with the Party the hypothesis of jumping to the street. But this possibility, too, needed to be studied.

Picking up on this idea, and with Filipe's agreement, in the next message out to the Party they posed some new questions. Where, with more precision, did the ledge end? At what distance from the roof? Mid-air? Near any window to the attic? At what distance from the last grated windows of the 3rd Floor?

Two weeks later, the response came. The stone ledge ended at the neighboring building next to the stairway skylight.

15

"The saw?" Vítor asked António. "You said to leave that to you. Did you take care of it? How?"

"Take it easy, Vítor. I already have it." The truth is, he already had it when they transferred him from Peniche to the 3rd Floor.

At the Fort they were also planning an escape. At that time the Party had sent him the saw. Not in a cake baked for that purpose, nor hidden in a bag of clothes. Those methods had already been discovered and couldn't be counted on. It was inside a pair of shoes with an inner sole. He had it right now on his feet. In his locker he kept another pair of shoes, saving them for the time when he'd have to dismantle this pair to retrieve the saw.

"So take it easy, Vítor," he repeated. "I already have it."

Vítor was not satisfied with this response. They would have to look at length into various questions: first, the size of the saw. Eventually, some kind of wooden handle to protect the fingers. The places on the window bars to be sawn. How to cancel out or diminish the noise. Calculate how many days it would require to saw the bars on the chosen window.

And not only would they have to study all these questions but begin without any loss of time, because it would certainly take many days to complete such work. António agreed.

One thing was a given: The most complicated and daring scheme was now the only one considered possible, that is, tiptoeing along the stone ledge to the neighboring building.

Like Vítor, Filipe still had some doubts about this plan. "Maybe too difficult," he voiced.

"At least you're saying 'difficult' and not 'impossible,'" António replied. "Come with me." And he proposed a visit to the washroom. Filipe would see how António did it, and he could try doing the same.

"With the two of us inside, we'll have to be very quick so no one enters and surprises us. You'll see how I do it. And then, when you try it too, I'll stand outside and cough to signal that someone's coming."

António dexterously repeated his experiment for his comrade. "Did you have a good look? Pressed to the wall, head to foot, palms spread on the wall at shoulder height, and advancing, sliding your feet angled against the wall, toes out, heels in, as though you were on that stone ledge the comrades told us about."

"I don't know if I can."

"If you're not afraid of heights, I'm sure you can do it."

He left Filipe by himself. No one appeared. After a short time, Filipe came out.

"It's amazing. If that's the way it's going to be, it'll be a cinch."

"A cinch no, but we will do it," António corrected.

16

This had never happened before: Chagas parading through the 3ʳᵈ Floor, now side by side chatting with Garcia.

If he had come out of the Room for this kind of conversation, it was certainly because he did not have absolute confidence in the others there.

The appearance of these two gave rise to protest, rumor and the odd expression of disfavor.

"What the hell does this guy want here?" Beja of the white beard asked. "Surely not just to take a walk."

Feeling profound disgust seeing his comrade in apparent conspiracy with the informer, Augusto avoided any contact and stood with other comrades near one of the barred windows.

"What's wrong with you?" Inácio asked, noticing his comrade's turmoil.

"That man is about to turn traitor," he murmured barely audibly.

Told who it was accompanying Chagas, they all quickly grasped the situation. No question, making friends with

Garcia and saying he wanted to help him, Chagas was trying to pry out what the PIDE couldn't.

Understanding this, the comrades immediately initiated their plan of action. They organized themselves in such a way as always to have a group of them as close as possible to the two so they could not speak freely.

The scene became ridiculous. Walking back and forth from one side to another, Chagas and Garcia were constantly surrounded by comrades, almost bumping into them, and always listening.

For the first few minutes that's all it was, but then they started having fun with it. The slurs, laughs and jokes at their expense multiplied.

Chagas saw that he did not command the terrain there that would allow him to reach his objective. He interrupted his promenade with Garcia, and they retreated to the Room without appearing to be scurrying back.

Upon disappearing through the doorway, they could hear a round of applause and laughter to celebrate the 3rd Floor victory.

The locks clanged in the grated gate and the metal-plated door, and two guards entered, billy-clubs in their fists. They shouted, "What's going on here?"

Nothing was going on. Life on the 3rd Floor had returned to normal, and no one gave them any explanation.

That afternoon, at visiting time, António's wife brought clean clothes, and there was a cigarette paper message hidden in the placket.

By curious coincidence, although long delayed, the Party was responding to what the 3rd Floor had communicated about Augusto's heroic behavior with the police, and his fear that Garcia might sing.

There was no need for concern. Everything those two knew about safe houses, support contacts, railway stations utilized by the comrade in the leadership—who had successfully escaped—all had been modified, with no remaining trace.

"We'll have to let Garcia know," Vítor suggested.

Augusto disagreed with that idea. "Leave it alone. It's always valuable to see how he comports himself. The Party will get to know him better."

17

With Vítor now eliminated from participation in the escape plan, the three comrades considered the possibility of adding a third comrade with António and Filipe. It had to be someone completely trustworthy, physically agile, capable of balancing himself and sliding along the stone ledge across the whole length of the building, and without vertigo. And clearly, also someone who wanted to escape from prison to continue the struggle underground.

Augusto was the first name they thought of. But then they recalled the extreme nervousness and anxiety that the Garcia affair had brought out in him.

Another was Alberto, Party functionary and part of the *Avante!* distribution system. He acted valiantly with the police, and showed both strong combativeness and self-confidence.

There were many other comrades on the 3ʳᵈ Floor. With several it was known that they had comported themselves well facing the PIDE. The young Inácio had demonstrated uncommon qualities. Of the others, not much was known for certain. They all participated in the struggles on the Floor. But to include someone in an escape involving so much responsibility, they didn't see another comrade of that caliber.

"We can't lose more time," António insisted. "Either we go ahead just the two of us, Filipe and me, or we decide very soon on a third comrade. Let's talk to Alberto. I don't see anyone else."

He himself spoke with the comrade.

He told him there were plans being made for an escape. Only a small number of comrades knew, and others didn't need to know. "Do you want to join us? Do you feel you have the courage for it? Are you committed to returning to underground work?"

Alberto heard the proposal with quiet enthusiasm. He was favorably disposed toward it and, whether he participated in it or not, he wouldn't say a word to anyone, of that they could be assured. But to better evaluate the plan and his role in it, either they should definitively tell him, "Come with us" and he would go, or tell him what more it was necessary to do.

Little by little, António brought him up to date on the project.

"Hey, that's harder, " Alberto said.

"Are you ready to take this risk?"

"To risk, yes, but I'm not sure if I'm capable."

As he had done with Filipe, António brought him into the washroom, leaned face forward against the wall, palms extended at shoulder level, one foot after the other, toes out, heels in, and shifted himself a few meters.

"Try it. I'll wait outside. If anyone comes, I'll cough. If they see you doing this they'll think you're crazy. Or they'd get suspicious, which is worse."

He left and waited. Alberto took far longer than expected. What was he doing? Impatient, António was getting set to go in and see what was happening, when the comrade came out smiling.

"I never imagined it would be that easy. It's really fun. I did it four times. I'm in. Count on me."

Having decided in principle how the escape would go, and who would be in on it, they still had further important aspects to consider.

They had not yet examined a serious problem: passing in front of the Room as they moved along the ledge. They would no longer have the support of their hands on the façade of the building, and would have to proceed stepping for a few meters while holding onto the bars of the Room window, later to resume their movement leaning on the wall.

António spoke peremptorily: They would not desist on account of that problem. "It's one more risk, but we can't back down."

"Clearly," Alberto said.

"Decided," Vitor concluded.

18

Once they resolved to commence sawing the bar on the window, they had to think about what time of day to do it. The last meal was at six-thirty. At eight, the guard's round, then silence. They just had to wait for the inmates to settle down so they could take good advantage of the time until the midnight round.

Vítor had studied where to start cutting—in the lower left corner of the grate. And it was he who initiated the work.

He rose cautiously from his bed and rapidly, decisively, applied saw to metal to make the first cuts. He stopped right away. In the silence on the Floor, the sharp sound of the saw resonated unmistakably. At that rate it wouldn't be long before they'd be discovered. Without needing to explain to António and Filipe, who were by his side, he put away the saw, got into bed and drew his blanket over him.

The next morning the three comrades discussed what to do, stepping out onto an uncertain road of speculation, dread, and failure in their attempt.

They tried to soften the sound by smearing the saw with oil. The sound became less acute, but just as perceptible. They would start sawing and, after two or three movements, suspend work for a few moments. Then they realized, thinking shrewdly, that if some inmate were awake, the steady intervals of sound would heighten his expectation of continuity.

They proceeded, without really finding a solution, until an unexpected occurrence opened up new possibilities. One night, shortly after the eight o'clock round, came an echo from the street—the overpowering sound of dance music, obviously from some popular group in the neighborhood.

"Now providence is with us!" Filipe laughed.

"As long as it continues, let's take full advantage," said Vítor.

So they did, and day by day, the sawing of the bars advanced, alongside constant tremors of foreboding.

More than once, one prisoner or another got up to go to the bathroom, and at the same natural pace, returned to his bed. One night, though, something else happened. Whoever it was took a few steps and stopped for a beat or two, appearing to turn toward the grated window the comrades were sawing. They suspended work immediately and made no move. The figure made one more slow step and then went to the washroom. On his return, he repeated this strange behavior. Could he have discovered what they were doing?

They redoubled their caution. On the following nights, however, the incident did not repeat itself, and they never found out who this curious man was.

The deepest cause of tension, however, came not from the comrades' moving about, but from the guards' vigilance. The cuts in the iron that they were making were disguised with plugs of bread dough tinted by rust and ink that they molded into the cut. This was scary, because on their rounds, the guards checked the bars with a metal object they tapped on the grating to detect any different timbre.

At each of those moments the comrades held their breaths in profound, terrified expectation. Otherwise firm, confident and decisive, they also experienced intensely this violent torrent of emotions. And so it was, up to the last day, up to the last minute.

19

The bolts and metallic sounds of opening gate and metal-plated door resounded on the 3rd Floor. The lights went on, and the guards on their midnight round paced amongst the beds, feeling the blankets here and there to verify the prisoners' presence, and tapping with metal against the window grates.

Noticing nothing out of the ordinary, they withdrew, noisily closing the gate and door, and shutting off the lights. The 3rd Floor fell again into tranquility and peace, as if nothing was happening. Only the faint light from the street muted the darkness.

In their beds, next to the last barred window, António, Filipe and Vítor prepared for the fateful moment. Alberto had quietly come over to join them and stretched out on one of the beds, covering himself with a blanket.

Owing to the lightheadedness and vertigo that he suffered, Vítor would not be one of the fugitives. Still, he had done much of the preparatory work and played an all-important role. He was the one who for the most part sawed the bars, and now it was up to him to complete this long labor, opening the way for his comrades to pass.

They still had to wait, however.

The midnight round had passed. It had been established that only around one hour later, comrades would be waiting on the roof of the neighboring building, at the end of the narrow stone ledge along which the three had to walk.

For unending minutes, emotions contained, they sat with cool serenity waiting for the moment to carry out their escape. Across the wide space of the 3ʳᵈ Floor spread a thick pregnant resonance. Someone got up and softly padded to the bathroom.

In no other place were the immobility and silence so profound as on those beds next to the last grated window.

Soundlessly, Vítor finished sawing the bars. The other comrades removed their blankets and sat up. Vítor gave the signal. He lightly touched each comrade, one, two, three, to make sure they were awake and ready.

The long-awaited time had come.

With studied intent, Vítor removed the sawn bars and, opening up the space to the cool night air, he gave a silent farewell to each in the agreed-upon order.

António left first, Alberto next, and Filipe last.

Vítor listened carefully. Quiet on the Floor, complete quiet outside. With a fearful feeling of vertigo, he imagined his comrades pacing themselves from moment to moment at third-floor height, along the stone ledge, just as he had seen them training in the washroom. Body against the building wall, arms open at shoulder level, supportive palms along the wall, feet always toes out, heels in, gently shuffling across the narrow stone ledge, with no rush or impatience, slowly, slowly, calm of mind and confident. He imagined them now passing by the Room, holding onto the window grates, and proceeding anew leaning against the façade. One false step, one uncoordinated move, one twitch, a sudden, unexpected attack of dizziness, and it would be a fall from the heights and death to all three.

By now they would have had time to reach the roof of the adjacent building, where comrades were waiting for them. From outside, only fresh air and silence. More time passed: complete and soothing silence.

With the deep contentment that flooded his every pore, Vítor lay down on his bed, covered himself with his blanket and tried in vain to sleep, waiting for the four a.m. round.

20

With the four o'clock round, the lights went up. The two guards advanced onto the Floor without noting anything extraordinary—every prisoner covered with his blanket, and no suspicious moves.

Near the end of the Floor, a short distance from the grated window, they broke out in panic. An enormous hole in the grate opened the way out, to the city, to the open air.

Loud alarm whistles blew, with appeals for help. Pistols in hand, the flustering guards flitted from side to side in the hall. The prisoners awoke in shock, not knowing what was happening.

In a minute, more guards brandishing billy-clubs invaded the Floor and blocked the exit.

"You there!" they shouted at Vítor, still covered by his blanket and pretending to sleep. "Don't you hear?" they demanded, yanking him out of his bed with blows.

"Where are your comrades?" they asked, now noticing their absence.

The question itself, absurd as it was, confirmed the success of the escape.

"I didn't see anything," Vítor responded. His joy was so great that he barely felt the blows they inflicted on him.

On the Floor, disorder and confusion reigned. Some guards ordered prisoners to get up from their beds, while others said no one should make a move.

Beja of the white beard was among the first to understand what happened. "Some comrades escaped," he said in a low voice to his neighbor in the next bed.

"Who?" his neighbor asked immediately.

Waving his billy-club, the head guard arrived. All movement stopped, awaiting orders. "Put your beds up!" he shouted. "And everyone in line for the count-off."

They got in line and the chief guard himself counted them three times.

Suddenly he lifted his baton and unleashed a general thrashing. The guards needed no pretext whatsoever to beat them all.

Rising above the guards' shouting, the prisoners' protest, a valiant but futile gesture at self-defense, echoed throughout the whole prison.

The only guards who remained in place, their hands on their pistol holsters, stood next to the last window, as though they feared that other prisoners might escape through it.

Finally the riot ended. The guards remained watchful, the prisoners taking stock of their wounds, alive with joy at their comrades' escape.

Vítor, blood running from the blows on his head and scalp, was calm and happy, a smile on his lips. Augusto stood with his arms crossed, indifferent to the wounds on his face that he had suffered in the brutal aggression. Beja, stroking his beard with a wide grin, was surely cogitating on some commentary he'd make. Inácio, with the boyish face, stood straight, almost at attention. Rudolfo, face bruised from the blows, stood with his hands akimbo as if in defiance.

One thing was for sure: The escape succeeded. The fugitives had gained their freedom. The whole collective of prisoners adopted the success as their own victory.

Hours passed since the four o'clock round. The head guards and some of the others had withdrawn. Daylight was already filtering onto the 3rd Floor, and everything seemed at a halt waiting for what would come.

The morning hours grew, and there were no aides, no coffee or crusts of bread.

"Hey, comrades!" a voice was heard. "This will serve to keep us slim, right?" Some answered with laughter.

With the reinforced guard on watch and ready to move, the prisoners went to the washrooms one by one to address their wounds, however possible. Later, under threatening vigilance, they tried to revert to their usual life—going to the toilet, walking on the Floor, gathering in groups to talk. The guards did not react.

Only when Inácio approached the first grated window on the Floor and prepared to offer breadcrumbs to the pigeons did the guard intervene: "Away from there! You can't be next to the window."

Again the voice of some wisecracker could be heard: "Take a look at this, comrades. Now they're afraid Inácio, too, is going to saw the bars and escape."

The lunch hour had passed with no meal when the gate and plated door opened loudly, and two men in street clothes entered the Floor. The guards on duty gave them respectful passage.

They went to the window through which the three comrades had escaped, closely examined the hole opened up by the sawn bars, and looked out. "I don't understand," one said to the other. "There's no way they could have lowered themselves to the street. They would have fallen right in front of the guardhouse and the sentinel. I just don't see how they disappeared."

The two men walked through the Room, looked inside the dining hall and the bathrooms and left.

Midmorning, two guards entered and headed to the Room, remaining there for some time. Then they left, removing in tow all the prisoners there, with suitcases and bundles in their hands. Chagas hurried out. Garcia followed, looking ashamed.

At twelve, the guards returned for their regular round, and at four, another round. No food, nothing eventful.

At nightfall, the head guard came back. The grated gate and the plated door were left open. They ordered a lineup. Prisoner after prisoner, one by one, were called to leave. One way or another, they all found a way of saying goodbye to those remaining.

"Courage, comrades!" "I'll see you all again some day!" "*A luta continua*—the struggle continues!" "Long live the PCP!" These were among the farewell phrases heard.

The last ones called were Vítor and Augusto, who left together.

Much later the fate of almost all of them was learned. Vítor and Augusto, along with Valdo, whom the PIDE had sent to Peniche, were placed in dungeons until they were shipped off to the Fort of Angra do Heroismo in the Azores. Inácio and Rudolfo went to the Fort of Peniche. Some, like the three singers from Alentejo, were freed. The rest went to the South Stronghold at the Fort of Caxias.

Waiting for repairs, the 3rd Floor remained deserted—colder and sadder in the absence of an honorable collective of men persecuted but confident in the future. And also because the pigeons stopped flying to its grated windows, no longer finding there a friendly palm offering bread.

Struggle and Life

Preface by Álvaro Cunhal

WHEN the volume of stories *Os Corrécios* (The Slackers) was published at the end of 2002, under the name Manuel Tiago, it was my intention that it would be the last book of stories.

But the enjoyment of writing fiction is an irrepressible need. And with no specific plans for the future, I started writing individual episodes of the Party's struggle in forced hiding. The work proceeded over time, growing, making connections, exciting the imagination and, little by little, this story, now published, came out [2003].

[The present edition in English translation combines two separately published books, *Sala 3 e Outros Contos* and this story, *Lutas e Vidas. Os Corrécios* (*The Slackers and Other Stories*) will shortly appear from International Publishers.]

1

Quite early one morning, after watching for the signal that he could approach the house, Valdo abandoned his car and went to knock on the door. Leonel and Constança let him in, nervous over this unplanned visit.

Valdo went straight to the point that brought him there in such a hurry.

On the road that Leonel traveled by bicycle for the work he was doing restructuring the party organization, police patrols were stopping cyclists to identify and interrogate them. Surely they were looking for Leonel, who urgently needed to move to another house and start working with other local cells.

Leonel interrupted him: "Abandon the cells? And if we leave this house, where will we go?"

Valdo reassured him. The Secretariat, of which he was part, had taken measures to replace him, and had a plan for exactly where Leonel should go find a house the next day: Cela Velha, near Alcobaça. A lot of emigrants went abroad from there, and there were many houses left behind. If he could get one, he should immediately move in.

"And Constança?"

Valdo answered the question. "Set your watch to my time. At four this afternoon, I'll be waiting for you by the station at Cela Nova. There's a road to Cela Velha there. We'll see what to do then, whether or not you've already secured a house."

He was told not to worry about Constança. Valdo would take care of that.

Leonel lost no time. He grabbed his bicycle and got on the road. He had good strong legs and arrived in Cela Velha by mid-morning.

He headed for a grocery shop. At the counter were a heavyset man and a slender woman with a pleasant face.

"Can you tell me if there are houses for rent around here? I was told many emigrants left their houses abandoned."

The man shrugged his shoulders crudely. Yes, there were closed-up houses. But the emigrants would be coming back for Christmas. You couldn't count on any of them.

"There aren't any others?"

The grocer looked the newcomer up and down: "I don't think so."

Just as Leonel was set to leave, the woman practically shouted, "Wait!"

She told him that Dona Maria Pedrosa owned a villa with a separate house where her brother had lived. But he died, and since then the house remained empty.

"You're crazy, Isabel," said the grocer, eyeing Leonel from head to toe and the bicycle leaning by the door. "A house like that is not for this man, not for someone of his type."

The woman did not give in. She left the counter and accompanied Leonel to the door, pointing to a home at the end of the street. "There. Knock on the door and ask for Dona Maria Pedrosa."

Leonel followed her advice, propped up his bicycle and knocked on the door. A maid opened it, and he asked for the mistress. The lady took a while, but at last came out to speak with him.

She was a woman of a certain age, of a quiet demeanor and dressed in black. Leonel said why he had come.

"No," she started. The house was closed, and she had no thought of renting it.

"I looked elsewhere, but they told me the emigrants' houses aren't for rent. The only closed and unoccupied one is the one you have at your villa."

Dona Maria mulled it over, gazing directly at Leonel.

"And you really need to live here in this area?"

"Yes, for my situation, this is the place that serves me best."

"Wait a moment," Dona Maria replied calmly.

She disappeared inside for a while, reappearing with a light shawl on her head. She had visibly fixed herself up to go out. "Let's go."

And with Leonel by her side wheeling the bicycle by hand, they walked to the courtyard.

There, spread over a spacious lot, were a well with a levered well pole and bucket, a garden shed, a tank for washing clothes, a tiny doghouse and a narrow building whose door Dona Maria opened. Suspended from the ceiling, with a rope to release the water, was a pail.

"My brother," she said, "always took a cold-water shower."

The house had windows at the front. The entrance was at the back through the kitchen. Rooms led from one to the next, without a corridor, with windows only on the courtyard side. First a good-sized kitchen with an enormous table, hanging pots and pans, cupboards for china and tableware and drawers for towels. Then came a modestly furnished room with a long table, a few chairs and a bookcase without books. On the table stood an oil lamp. And finally, two bedrooms, one with a double bed and a large armoire, the other with only a bed.

"That's it," said Dona Maria.

"And the rent?" Leonel asked almost in shock.

"I'll rent it to you just to bring life back to the house, like my brother. You'll see how much you can pay. I believe in people. Treat the house nicely for me is all I ask."

Leonel told her what he was paying for the house he had been living in. It wasn't much, but Dona Maria didn't object. "That's all right, then."

Leonel wanted to pay three months in advance. It was the first time Dona Maria smiled.

"There's no need to be in such a rush."

They exited the house. Dona Maria handed over the key, asking further, "And your family?"

"My wife. I'll bring her tomorrow with my things."

"Children?"

"No, we don't have children."

Dona Maria stayed silent and thoughtful for a few moments. "I have two orphan children in my house. They're good company and bring joy to the house," she explained.

She stood surveying the property, where a caretaker was tending a huge garden. Then she retreated with slow steps.

Leonel went back in again. He sat at the kitchen table eating the bread and cheese Constança had prepared for him, then went to lie down for a bit, since he still had some hours before riding his bicycle to the meeting place with Valdo at four.

He was punctual, and Valdo was waiting at the designated spot. He didn't waste time. He led Leonel to his car and maneuvered the bicycle into the trunk.

"Let's swing by the house so that later today, or tomorrow, when I make the move and bring Constança, I'll know the way."

2

Leonel found a blanket and lay down, waiting anxiously for his comrades' arrival. Only late into the night did he fall asleep, but deeply.

When he awoke, mid-morning already, he went outside, upset that the comrades had not arrived yet. The air was clear and bright. Across the compound, maybe fifty meters away, the caretaker was working the garden.

At last they arrived. Constança was greatly pleased with the house, which she walked through from end to end. Afterward, she lit the oil stove and put water on to boil for coffee.

Valdo and Leonel sat at the table in the other room.

"You're going to help out with the restructuring of two cells. One is in the cement factory halfway to Marinha Grande, and the other in the glass factories in Marinha Grande. I know you'll do well. The Party reorganization that we're completing now requires a lot of effort from all of us.

"Over the years, these cells have engaged in important struggles, and also suffered profound blows. Now, with the reorganization of 1942-43, the Party Secretariat has stabilized, and once again, to various degrees, the organization is taking hold and developing in the whole country. It's happening in the cement factory and also in the glass industry of Marinha Grande, which falls to you to guide them."

"Who's giving me the contacts?"

"Pay close attention to what I'm going to explain. On Thursday, which is the day the comrades meet, at five o'clock sharp, the hour the workday ends, you should be standing by the front gate of the cement factory, and on the next Thursday at the front gate of the Carlos Gallo bottle factory in Marinha Grande. Be at the workers' exit. You'll be approached by a worker who will ask you if you're waiting for someone. You respond—take note—'it's been more than an hour,' and the other will say, 'All things come to him who waits.' Then he will lead you to a house where they meet. It'll be exactly the same at both places. Is everything clear? Do you have any questions?"

"It's all clear. I've taken note."

They were about to continue the conversation when Constança entered with a coffee pot, sugar and slices of bread with cheese.

They interrupted their talk and ate their little meal appreciatively. When they had eaten, Leonel asked if there weren't other cells in the region. Yes, there were. In Marinha Grande, there's a comrade who, for professional reasons, used to make the rounds to a lot of places, and he had some contacts. Comrades there would give him information.

"When will I meet you again?" Leonel inquired.

"We're not going to set another meeting at this time," Valdo answered. "I will find a way to appear at the right time."

They stood up, and Valdo said goodbye.

"Don't you want lunch?"

No, he had to be on his way. As he left, they embraced, he got into his car and left. The two comrades followed him with their eyes until the car disappeared out the villa driveway to the road.

3

At five o'clock, following Valdo's instructions, Leonel stood at the front gate of the cement factory waiting for the employees to leave. Many had already left when, finally, a young worker came over to talk with him.

"Are you waiting for someone?"

"It's been more than an hour."

"All things come to him who waits."

The pre-arranged words having been spoken, the young man took Leonel's arm. "Come with me, comrade."

He led him to a somewhat isolated house on a street in town and opened the door.

"Go in, comrade. I'll put your bicycle away."

He saw an entrance foyer, a corridor and a kitchen. "My name is Leonel," said the visitor.

"Have a seat. I'll prepare some coffee for us. My companion Joana isn't here yet. She's a Party member, too, and is employed in a little workshop that closes later."

After the coffee, the comrade turned up his shirtsleeves, put a kettle of water on the oil stove and began peeling potatoes.

"I'm putting everything together for our dinner. It's cod. I know you'll like it."

When Joana arrived, they'd finish preparing the meal. She wouldn't be too much longer now. They'd have time to enjoy dinner without rushing. The leadership of the cell would gather at night there in the house.

They sat at the table, Leonel writing on sheets of paper and the young comrade reading a newspaper.

Joana came, they ate and awaited the other comrades in the cell Secretariat, who appeared before long. One strong man, middle-aged, and another as young as the man of the house, who introduced Leonel and then the other comrades, José and Fernando.

"And you?" Leonel asked. "You haven't told me your name yet."

He begged his pardon and said his name was Carlos.

Before beginning the meeting, Carlos asked, "And Joana? What do you say? Couldn't she join us?"

After a moment of hesitation, it was José who answered. "Today, yes, but not as a regular practice."

They agreed, and the meeting began.

It was again José who led off, a calm, serious man in contrast to the cheerful vivacity of the two younger fellows.

He reported that as a result of the reorganization, there were now ten comrades who belonged to the cell. They weren't so many in a factory with hundreds of workers, but they had a recognizable influence on everyone. He described how the Secretariat established contacts with the workers.

"Carlos, tell us what the problems are that the workers are facing, and Fernando, say how we are guiding the struggle."

The main problem right now, Carlos reported, are the low wages with no raise for a long time. Prices had risen a great deal, and therefore real wages had declined. He brought forward many concrete points. Yet other reasons for discontent included the poor quality of lunch in the factory dining hall.

After that summary, José called on Fernando, who spoke, like Carlos, in a very lively, upbeat manner. They tried to elevate the workers' consciousness and give orientation to the general discontentment. They were listened to with keen interest. Often the workers sought them out for a clarification or opinion. They were anticipating the unfolding of a general movement for demands, but things were not mature enough yet for that.

"You, Joana," José asked, "do you want to say something?"

Yes. In the little factory where she worked, there were very few employees. But among them was another woman in the Party, and the two of them were available to help the cement workers with propaganda work.

"There you have it, comrade," José said to Leonel. "Give us your opinion and also tell us something about the situation nationally with the Party."

Leonel spoke in a quiet, clear voice with many pauses. He was pleased, from what he had heard, that the Party cells, after the reorganization, had influence. He appreciated the analysis and information provided by the cell leadership. Concerning the general situation of the Party, he said that according to what he could tell, it was in a phase of broad reorganization and expansion, with growing influence.

It was already late, and the meeting ended. They agreed to meet in two weeks. José and Fernando left.

"You can sleep here, Leonel," Carlos said. "Get up and leave as you wish. Just pull the door and close it. I have the key. But anyway, we don't have robberies around here. I'll leave something to eat on the table. Come here, I'll show you where I put your bicycle."

They wished him good night. Leonel slept well, ate his breakfast, washed his dish in the kitchen, grabbed his bicycle, closed the door and departed. The return trip back to the house was long and tiring, but he was used to that.

4

A week later, at the same hour, Leonel was at the gate to the Carlos Gallo bottle factory in Marinha Grande. A comrade came up to him and with surprise exclaimed, "You here? We were together at the Third Congress, the first we held in secret."

"Come give me a hug, Vasco. I'm amazed it should be specifically you who'd be waiting for me."

"It's a little long from here to my house. I live next to the railway station. But we have time to get there in time for dinner."

They chatted along the way and arrived at the house only a few steps away from the station. His companion, Marisa, a worker in the packing department and also a member of the local committee, had just returned home and was fixing dinner.

Vasco set the bicycle aside.

They ate hungrily and continued talking, expecting the other comrades. Vasco said the organization of work in the glass factories was very complex. At the meeting about to take place, the other comrades would explain.

Tomás and Abel arrived on time, and everyone was introduced. They said where they worked and what jobs they performed—Vasco and Marisa at the Carlos Gallo bottle factory. Abel, a very young and vivacious fellow, was at the New Factory, which produced articles for everyday use, but he also had a contact at the Marquês de Pombal factory, which had hundreds of workers. Tomás was at Emílio Gallo. In all these factories, Party and Communist Youth organizations were quite important. They all gave their support to the reorganization in several other factories.

"We have to explain to you now," Vasco said, "how work in the glass industry is organized so you can better understand how to develop our activity and our struggles."

He explained that the work is done by "teams" composed of seven or eight workers from the official down to the apprentices. Wages for the adults were based on the number of pieces produced, which meant an inhuman speedup in the work rhythm. The apprentices received miserable wages and suffered bad treatment and physical punishment besides.

"That's it, comrade, that's how the work is organized in the industry, and the conditions under which we conduct our activity."

Abel spoke next. With the reorganization, above all since 1942, the Party got stronger—and unexpectedly quickly. It was possibly stronger and more influential than ever before in its history.

"Look, comrade. Just a few days ago, at the New Factory, where I am, there was an apprentice strike. If the apprentices stop work, the officials don't receive the fused glassware that the apprentices transport, and they're forced to stop, too. That's what happened. And the apprentices won satisfaction for their demands."

"What's happening at the New Factory is happening in others, too," Tomás added. "At Emílio Gallo, there was also a struggle going on, led by the Party and the Communist Youth."

Vasco wanted to add a few words. "We've been talking about our area and our struggles. But we've all emphasized what's been happening in the Party since the reorganization, and particularly what's happening on the level of national leadership and the big initiatives they're making. I myself, like you, was sent by our local committee to the Third Congress in 1943.

"Can you tell us anything more about the current situation?"

Leonel began by referencing and appreciating the comrades' reports at this meeting about the kinds of activity the organization was conducting in Marinha Grande. He recalled that the Third Congress had taken place right after the big strikes in the Lisbon region, and the notable advances, thanks to the Party, in the national anti-fascist movement. The new Secretariat was showing its capacity for guiding this work and resisting repression. The Party was positioned to shortly obtain some new and important successes.

And so went Leonel's first meeting with the local committee of Marinha Grande.

They set their next meeting to take place in three weeks.

Tomás and Abel excused themselves and left.

Before going to bed, Vasco warned Leonel that he'd likely wake up in the middle of the night to the sound of clanging rail cars, as the freight train passed through here and made a number of switches in the station.

"If the noise wakes you up, don't worry if you see me get up and go outside for a little fresh air. It's an old habit of mine when it's good weather, like today. Marisa sleeps through it all. She never wakes up when I go out."

When Leonel awoke, Vasco and Marisa had already left for work. He ate a little breakfast that his comrades had set out for him and mounted his bicycle to return home.

5

Leonel was away, and Constança was washing clothes in the tank. The caretaker stepped away from his work and calmly walked toward the house.

They exchanged greetings, and he said he was just going to the garden shed where he had a sack of manure for fertilizer. It didn't take him long, but he made no move to leave. He stood not far from Constança, and finally said what he had come for. He introduced himself as Francisco. Dona Maria had instructed him to bring to the house everything they needed from the garden. Having said that, he still did not leave. There was something else on his mind, which eventually spilled out.

You must feel very alone in the house at times when your husband is gone. What you miss is having a dog with you, if for nothing more than to bark at night as warning that someone was approaching the house.

In town, he had a little house and many dogs. He liked dogs very much, and he could bring her one.

Constança accepted the offer, and the next day he appeared with it. It surprised her to think this was really a dog, such a tiny, skeletal little animal.

"It's a little puppy," Francisco explained. "It's skinny, but once she gets a little meat on her bones, she'll be a very sweet doggie."

Right away, Leonel disagreed. "You shouldn't have accepted it."

What to do? Constança had to keep it.

It stayed with her, she fed it as much as possible, and the puppy grew. What a figure she cut! When she ate, she looked strange: her head against her chest and her front legs to one side, her back legs to the other side, and in the middle her enormous belly. You could cry and laugh at the same time.

After a few weeks, the caretaker returned. Her dog was in heat, and any day now Constança would have a pack of male dogs on her doorstep. He wouldn't permit that, so he took the little dog away and promised another.

"Let's see what you bring me now," Constança warned.

He wished he could offer her more, but his little house had a tiny back yard with another bitch expecting another litter, and then he'd bring her a cute male puppy.

But the story repeated itself—a skeletal little creature she fattened up, the big belly surrounded by bones.

When he returned home, Leonel again criticized Constança. She should have refused. It looked as though the caretaker were playing them for fools.

For some days, Francisco didn't come to the house and nor did he care to talk about it. Instead, by surprise, he brought a huge basket of vegetables and went away without saying a word.

One day, though, he returned, for the first time ever with a big smile on his face, followed by a beautiful male dog. "This is for you both. I'm offering him to you."

Leonel liked the animal. He and Constança ended up giving him the name "Dog" in English. In the morning, Dog left his little house and came scratching at the kitchen door. If the door was open a little, he'd put his paw on the threshold. Leonel or Constança would say, "No, Dog."

And Dog, ears pricked, then lowered, as if speaking, wouldn't enter.

One time Leonel returned home exhausted, slept soundly and only awoke when the sun was high. Bright morning light poured through the window. Constança appeared. "Lazy boy! Would you like me to bring you your coffee in bed?"

No, he'd get up. But could she first open the window for him? Constança did. A pleasant gust of fresh air came in.

"Dog!" Leonel called. "Dog!"

He responded immediately. Jumping with joy, he appeared on the windowsill, once, twice, three times, greeting his master with sweet barking.

Dog thus came to be dearly treasured. It seemed impossible that they had ever lived without him.

The fact that Constança had allowed herself to be deceived, without objection, by the offers of the two emaciated dogs had profound implications.

When she first met Leonel, she lived with two sisters. Their mother had died long before. Leonel was a neighbor, they got to know each other in a brief love affair and, when Leonel transitioned to underground work, she decided, with courage and love, to go with him.

The first house they lived in together, from which they moved to Cela Velha, sat in a well-populated area. Even when Leonel spent the night out, she felt surrounded by occupied houses, and that gave her a certain sense of security.

The situation changed radically with the move to the house at the villa. When Leonel did not come home to sleep, she felt abandoned in the wilderness at night and afraid. Yes, she was afraid.

During the day, she always went out to the town to make purchases, and was always graciously received by the grocer's wife, and even he treated her respectfully. Now, she was not the wife of the guy who showed up with his bicycle to look for a house. Now, she was the lady who lived in the house at Dona Maria Pedrosa's villa.

Days, if the weather was good, she'd occupy herself drawing water from the well, washing clothes and cooking. But at night she felt a terrible aloneness in an empty, dark and silent space that she found hard to bear.

It was no wonder she had accepted the offer of the skeletal dogs without reservation, in the hope of some company.

Finally, Dog came, and the sense that he was in his little doghouse softened her solitude somewhat.

6

One hot, sunny day, Leonel arrived at the cement factory mid-morning. The meeting started shortly.

He found a new situation: disagreements amongst the cell leadership about the progress of the struggle. The youngest members, Carlos and Fernando, argued that conditions already existed to successfully launch a strike for the demands they had been fighting for so long, but José was opposed to that line of thinking.

"The factory has hundreds of workers," he contested. "Our dozens of comrades are active and do have influence. But in my opinion, it would be premature before we hear from a much larger number of workers on this question."

"Every employee supports the demands we are putting forward. The conditions are ripe," said Carlos.

"If we wait to find out if hundreds of workers in the factory are for the strike," Fernando further underlined, "we'll never get there."

They suspended the meeting for a brief meal and resumed mid-afternoon. "What is your opinion, Leonel?" they asked.

"It's not easy giving an opinion," Leonel responded. "You comrades are the ones who have contact with the factory workers, you've spoken with them, you've gotten to know their disposition to strike. There's a lot to think about, given the views of Carlos and Fernando on the one hand, and José's on the other. In their view, they've confirmed the will and spirit for struggle in the factory. And in his, he sees the need to better feel out, and deepen the workers' attitude before the Party issues an appeal to strike and for our militants to stop work. So for that reason, I believe that before proceeding to a strike, the immediate need is to hear from the maximum number of workers possible. Hold meetings of the comrades. Place this task before them as the task for all members, and then, with a better grasp of the situation, if favorable, decide on the date for a strike and the appeal to all personnel to halt work."

The comrades agreed to this plan, the meeting ended, and Leonel got on his bicycle and headed home.

7

In Marinha Grande again, the meeting took place, as usual, at Vasco's house.

They reported significant advances in the organization, and rapid developments in the current struggles: many new Party members, contacts with and the creation of a sizable Party nucleus in Leiria. And one big surprise: Comrades from Vieira de Leiria at the Tomé Feteira File Factory had sought out the organization in Marinha Grande to announce that, considering the reorganization of the Party, they had established a cell there with enthusiastic comrades.

"We're considering forming a regional committee," Vasco announced.

The meeting over, the comrades asked Leonel if he could stay with them one more day. The next day the weather would be good, and the organization would hold their annual beach party at a spot to the north of São Pedro de Moel. For Leonel, it would be a festivity full of good fun, and all the comrades would be delighted if he'd participate.

"Very well," Leonel accepted, "although at my house, they'll be rather upset about my unexpected absence."

Abel and Tomás had left already, and Vasco, Leonel and Marisa sat down to dinner, talking some more until bedtime. Leonel fell into a profound sleep.

"I had to shake you several times to wake you up," said Vasco, pulling on the arm of a sleepy Leonel.

"Hnnnn?" he mumbled, not quite awake.

"It was hard!" Vasco continued, now smiling broadly.,

"Sorry, friend. I was wiped out, and yesterday was a long day."

It had been indeed. More than forty kilometers on his bicycle, and lengthy meetings well into the night.

He rose, stretched his arms, went to the bathroom, and when he got back to the main room, Vasco and Marisa had already prepared lunch.

"Everyone has lunch before we leave," Marisa said. "Later, on the beach, there will be more surprises, with another special treat. Here we'll just have cod and potatoes—it's ready, come to the table."

As she prepared the plates, she asked, "Would you like some garlic? I can slice it for you."

Leonel accepted, and they ate hungrily, along with a glass of wine.

"It's a magnificent day. You won't regret it."

After eating, as they sipped a fragrant, steaming coffee, Vasco explained: He and Leonel were invited guests. The people who organized the outing were two bottle factory workers, both Party members, the brothers João and António Boniné. When we arrive at the beach, you'll understand the reason, he said.

They left the house and shut the door. The sun was warm and bright.

"There they are," said Vasco.

A truck with an open carriage, carrying some thirty or forty workers, women included, was parked in front. They got on, joining the others, greeted everyone and settled in as best they could.

"Does anyone know when the Boniné brothers left?" Vasco asked.

"I saw them on the way in their pickup," a comrade answered.

"Is everyone here?" the driver asked.

"No," Vasco responded. "We still have to pick up Abel. Tomás can't come."

Arranging themselves in the carriage, they took off to retrieve one more comrade.

The highly agile Abel mounted in practically one jump, cheerily said hello to all, and confirmed that the Boninés had left hours before in their little truck.

8

After ten kilometers, passing through pine forest, they got to the heights over São Pedro de Moel and followed the road atop the coastal crags to the lighthouse.

On the curvy road, built long before human memory, they made their descent down the incline. They parked at the far end of the beach facing the ocean on a low dune composed of beaten sand hard as rock. The Boniné truck was already there.

"Here we are!" Vasco said, gesturing toward the beach, a wild, frightful, unsettling and uniquely mysterious locale.

A wide band of pure white sand, without a blemish, extended north until it disappeared from sight. The waves were high, the mighty, violent ocean tumbling forcefully, as if trying to conquer a sandhill at the water's edge, and gushing out into a long lagoon, finally dying away in low dunes the same color as the beach. The dunes emerged naturally out of the solid coastal lands. Right at the entrance to the beach, to a visitor's surprise, sat a dozen or so houses—not jerry-built barracks on the beach, but houses built to last with brick walls and cement, amongst which the largest and most distinguished was that of the Boniné brothers.

Throughout the course of the day, Leonel gradually learned the history of how this little community at Old Beach was constructed.

In Marinha Grande, the Boniné brothers were the only ones who owned a pickup, and they loved to drive it around. For years, they enjoyed their pastime of following the narrow road to Tercenas and other locales with acacia trees in the middle of the Leiria pine forests.

One summer day, they decided to go to São Pedro de Moel. They regretted it immediately. The beach belonged to the wealthy families of Marinha Grande industrialists. The extended Gallo and Roldão clans were arriving in a noisy cortege of luxury cars. The Boninés came, saw and left right away.

"This is not a place for us," António exclaimed.

"We have nothing in common with these people," said José. "Let's move on."

They continued driving along the road to the lighthouse. When they passed by it, the lighthouse keeper walked onto the road signaling for them to stop. "Where are you going?"

"To Old Beach," they informed him.

"Don't be crazy, my friends. Old Beach is cursed. It's no place to be, much less a place to relax. Don't let yourselves be deceived. It's a treacherous beach with moving sands. Years ago, a couple of people came this way and they wouldn't listen to me. They went down to it and remained there forever, swallowed by the shifting sands."

"Thanks for telling us that," the brothers said gratefully. "We'll be careful." And they went on their way.

It was the second time they stopped at Old Beach that the idea struck them to build a summer house there.

A number of other comrades followed them.

"But building on the beach isn't permitted," Leonel observed. "Didn't City Hall object?"

Yes, it did, he was told. Several times they threatened to go and knock down the settlement. But people resisted, so you still have these beautiful houses as the workers' summer retreat.

All this Leonel found out that day.

Arriving in the truck with the open carriage, Leonel, too, was enchanted, as the Boninés had been, by the grandeur and charm of the untamed beach.

They sat on the sand. "I see you had plenty to eat at lunch," João Boniné laughed. "Later we'll see if you have any room left for the acorn barnacles."

"That's the surprise," Vasco said. "This is the yearly festival for that delicious seafood."

Once again, the commanding Boniné voices rose. "Abel! Duarte! Your time has come! Go get those acorn barnacles!"

And turning toward a tall, beefy comrade, the other added, "Zé Pinto here is going with you to help. In the meantime, we'll put the water on to cook the barnacles."

With that, they lost no time and started setting a fire on top of the dune. They had brought everything they needed from Marinha Grande: two brick walls separated by a short span, pine needles in the sand, wood chips on top and, supported on the bricks, a strong metal grate. On top of that they placed an enormous pot of probably thirty liters. They filled it with water, put a lid on it and lit the fire. They tended the wood chips to make sure they were burning well. To one side sat two big piles of pine needles and wood chips.

Good swimmers both, Abel and Duarte started their fishing, with Zé Pinto's support.

The essential qualities were agility and courage. They made their descent down the cliff, tied to a rope that Zé Pinto had secured up top. When the waters swelled suddenly, propelled by the strong waves, the diver—now Abel, then Duarte—leaning on the rocks while the water still covered them, scraped a cluster of acorn barnacles from the stone. They repeated this action many times, filling sacks with the mollusks.

"Abel knows how to swim that well?" Leonel asked.

"He's a first-class swimmer, and very brave," Vasco told him.

An hour later, Abel and Duarte returned to the beach with their sacks full, which they emptied onto a big tarpaulin the Boninés had spread across the sand. One by one, the brothers put the barnacles in the pot of boiling water, and in under half an hour, the acorn barnacles were cooked.

The brothers emptied the water into the lagoon and distributed handfuls of barnacles to the crowd, who enjoyed them with an accompanying wine or beer. You just had to grab the tiny foot, lift the other end to your mouth and suck out the delicious shaft.

They passed the afternoon hours seated on the sand, happily nibbling, drinking and talking.

They gathered their things, closed the doors to the houses, said their goodbyes and took their places again in the truck with the open carriage. The Boninés and two or three other comrades remained behind to clean the beach and straighten up.

On reaching Marinha Grande, Abel, before he jumped down, embraced Leonel and Vasco.

Then it was Vasco, Marisa and Leonel's turn to get off the truck. They led Leonel to the house, Vasco handed him his bicycle, and asked, "Worth it, don't you think?"

"Yes, for me, too, it was a great party. I can't recall anything like it." They embraced.

"See you soon!"

"See you soon! I'll be back in two weeks."

Leonel mounted his bicycle, got on the road, and in just under three hours, arrived home.

He found Constança in an especially foul mood.

"Don't do this to me again, Leonel. You said you'd be home yesterday, and you didn't come. What was I supposed to think? That you'd been arrested, or what? I will not accept this, Leonel! I'm not going to take it any longer!"

And without waiting for a response, she went to bed.

"Constança!" Leonel wanted to explain. "I'm going to be home for two weeks now and not leave the house, do you hear?"

No response came. "Constança!" he insisted. She pretended not to hear.

9

Constança got up in a better mood, got dressed and didn't want to wake Leonel. She prepared breakfast and then, when she went into the bedroom again, she found him awake.

"Open the window for me," Leonel asked. She did so, and he called out, "Dog!"

Dog came and jumped up repeatedly, sprawling his front paws across the sill to see his master and bark.

Leonel got dressed, and they went to the kitchen to have breakfast, with the door to the compound open and Dog stationed with one paw poised at the entrance as though he wanted to enter.

They ate, gave the dog something to eat and got ready to go out and breathe some fresh morning air, when suddenly a young woman with a pleasant face appeared, saying she was Dona Maria Pedrosa's maid. The senhora had asked them to go over to the villa as soon as they could. And with that, she left.

"What does she want?" Leonel questioned.

"Does she want us to leave the villa?" asked Constança.

They put on nice clothes, combed their hair and started walking, with a gleeful Dog skipping alongside.

They were told to enter and, in a small room, Dona Maria received them accompanied by two boys.

"These are the two boys I told you about, Janito and Miguelito. They're my company, and the joy of this house." And she explained the reason why she had asked them to come to the villa.

The boys wanted to host a little party, so she made a cake and invited Leonel and Constança to take tea and share a slice with them. She thought, too, that not having children, they'd feel happy being at the party with these two boys.

"Clarinda!" she called. "Sit here with us at our little party. You, too, help me like a member of the family."

The young woman who had summoned them to the villa seated herself comfortably and participated, eating cake and drinking tea.

Moved as they were, Leonel and Constança didn't know what to say. But finally Leonel managed to find some words—how much he acknowledged and appreciated this generous invitation, and from his heart wished Dona Maria, for her kindness, and these two precious boys and Clarinda, good health and much happiness.

Constança also said a few words. "Dona Maria, dear lady, thank you for your example."

Dona Maria kissed them both and they said goodbye.

The boys led their guests to the door and were delighted to play with Dog a bit. More kisses and goodbyes.

And, glancing back as they retreated, Leonel and Constança looked at Dona Maria, Janito, Miguelito and Clarinda, signaling goodbye to them, waving their hands.

10

And so they passed their days, breathing the pure countryside air, reading, writing. All peaceful and quiet, finally, they had days on end to spend together.

Constança went out only to make purchases. They had tomatoes, peppers and vegetables in abundance, that the gardener brought by order of Dona Maria Pedrosa. In the stores, she bought bread, grocery items, meat and fish. She bought moderate amounts, but for two reasons, she was well served: first, because she paid cash, whereas most people put it on account. And second, because now for some time, she was the senhora who lived with her husband in the house at Dona Maria Pedrosa's villa.

The grocer, whom Leonel first approached to find a house to rent, was particularly obsequious. And Isabel, the grocer's wife, was sympathetic and friendly since the first moment when she had pointed Leonel toward the house at the villa. She greatly enjoyed conversing with Constança and sharing news of the surrounding area.

That day, there had been news indeed: A troupe of acrobat jugglers, a man, a woman and two boys. They played the drum to attract a crowd. The boys showed off their acrobatic tricks, while the woman went around collecting tips for the show from the spectators. The man exhibited an extraordinary feat.

"I don't understand it, Dona Constança, really I don't," Isabel confessed. "The man grabs a burning torch, turns his head up, and a huge flame comes out of his mouth."

With all her purchases, and this story, Constança returned home.

"I was getting nervous that you took so long," said Leonel.

Time passed calmly, until one night Constança was awakened by Dog's yelping—not his usual happy barks, but nervous, frenetic and angry. She woke Leonel. "Listen!" Constança said, "Someone's out there."

Leonel got up in one jump and the idea crossed his mind: *Was it the police? Had they traced their way to the house?*

"I'll see what it is!"

"Be careful, Leonel," Constança advised.

"Stay calm." Grabbing a lantern—and a pistol—he opened the door.

He almost had to laugh. A big, black dog was eating from Dog's dish, and Dog was answering it with fury.

With Leonel's arrival, and in the lantern light, the black dog ran away. Dog quieted down and gratefully ran to his master's legs.

"We got quite a shock," Leonel smiled.

So it went until one day, unexpectedly, Valdo showed up mid-morning to the house at the villa. He explained why he had come. The Party Secretariat had a new and very special job for Leonel. He needed to leave soon and try to finish his task in a maximum of two weeks.

Leonel interrupted. "Do we have to move from the house? And Constança?"

"No, you don't have to move. You can return here, and Constança can go with you."

This was the problem: Emídio, the comrade from the Coimbra region, who up to now had been the liaison with the Party Secretariat, had disappeared. The man in that region who was responsible for distributing the Party paper *Avante!*—a "highly responsible comrade"—had communicated the news. The organization was profoundly divided, the comrades in open conflict. It was an unsustainable situation, and everything had to be put back in order. If Emídio didn't fulfill his duties, he would have to be replaced. Leonel would go there as the delegate of the Party Secretariat, and take care of the matter within two weeks.

As for the house at the villa, they should pay three months in advance, and explain their temporary absence perhaps by saying a close relative had died and they were needed to help the family.

"I could say my mother died," Constança offered, though she had died many years before.

"And the dog?" an alarmed Leonel asked. "We can't abandon him—he'd die of hunger. Moreover, the people here, starting with Dona Maria, would find that extremely strange."

Valdo took his time answering. "You are still going to Marinha Grande. See if some comrade there can take him while you're away. If not, I'll keep him until you return. We'll have to think about what day you're leaving. I'll be back here tomorrow to decide on that."

"And transportation?"

"Naturally, we've thought about this. Clearly, for such a great distance, you can't go on bicycle. And it would be dangerous going by passenger train."

But they could go by freight train carrying merchandise, which travels the whole way only by night, stopping for a long time in each station. It has one car with a passenger compartment.

"Since you won't be taking bicycles to Coimbra, you'll have to go on foot to the Cela Nova station to pick up the freight train around nine p.m."

The departure date they chose was a weekday. They'd get out at the old station in Coimbra mid-morning the next day.

"You can have breakfast in the café at the station and pick up a commuter rail to the city. There you'll head to Sofia Street and find Model Books and Paper. The owner is a comrade and mornings he'll surely be by himself. You two enter, ask for Senhor Cesário and, confirming that it's him, tell him you're looking for him on account of Emídio. The comrade will then tell you what to do. Did you take note of everything?"

"Yes, everything's good."

"And you won't leave anything compromising in the house?"

"No, don't worry. I just have some notes, a few books, and some copies of *Avante!* But we'll take everything with us, as well as a change of clothes in a handbag."

"We'll be informed of your return," Valdo ended, "by the comrade distributing *Avante!* in Coimbra." He said goodbye and left.

Learning about the trip they were going on, Constança expressed herself with rare happiness. "Bravo! It'll be the first time I'll be going with you when you leave the house for work."

11

Leonel went again to Marinha Grande. The meeting was that night. The comrades were very excited. They had recruited a lot of new members to the Party and to the Communist Youth. The new members seemed full of spirit.

"The Party's been reborn, and we're overflowing with energy," Abel added.

"Listen, Vasco," Leonel said, before he left. "Now I have a favor to ask of you. I have a dog that I really love. You live here right next to the station, and you told me you always wake up when the freight train comes in. I'm going to be on that train in exactly two weeks. Could you come to the station so I can hand him off to you until I return?"

"Of course, my friend. I wouldn't refuse you anything."

"I'll let you know when I'm returning."

"Agreed."

12

Departure day came, and the time to leave the house to catch the freight train in Cela Nova. The evening before, they had gone to Dona Maria's villa to explain their absence.

They ate breakfast and picked up their bags with clothes and a briefcase containing a few books, notepads and copies of *Avante!* that were in the house.

At the kitchen door, Dog was waiting impatiently.

"Dog, my friend," said Leonel, stroking his pet. "You're going with us, but we have to part along the way."

Dog stiffened, then softened his ears as if understanding his master's words.

"Relax, friend," Leonel continued. "You're coming with us on the train and along the way, we'll leave you in good hands. It'll only be two weeks, and then we'll come get you."

They left, closing the door behind.

The freight train was already at the station. The metallic sound of clanging rail cars broke the general silence. The car with the passenger compartment was right at the front.

Leonel went quickly to buy their tickets. Without delay, they boarded the train and immediately hid Dog under the seat. "Be quiet, Dog, because you're not allowed to be here with us. But it's only until Marinha Grande."

The train stayed there for quite a while longer before it pulled out sluggishly toward the North.

At the Marinha Grande station, according to plan, Vasco was waiting. At the moment the train started up again, they handed Dog over to Vasco on the platform. The train left, but unexpectedly, Dog escaped from Vasco and started running alongside the track, trying to keep up with the train. Still running, he fell behind more and more as the train gathered momentum. Finally, Leonel, leaning out the window, saw him disappear into the darkness.

13

After a night of worrying about Dog's fate, they arrived, mid-morning, at the old station in Coimbra. They exited the train, had breakfast at the bar in the station and took the commuter rail to the new station. They asked how to get to Sofia Street and from there to Model Books and Paper.

Cesário was standing at the counter, expecting them. He greeted them and told them to accompany him by foot. He would lead in front. He lived close by, in a spacious, well-furnished house.

As soon as they arrived, he shouted, "Ivone!" and a young woman with a lovely face appeared, whom he introduced. "This is my wife. You, comrades, will be staying here in the house."

And when he and Leonel had to leave for work, Ivone would stay home with Constança for company.

Yes, they truly were very tired. They could sleep in a room Ivone showed them.

"I'm going to try tonight to get some of the comrades here who will bring you up to date on the situation," Cesário told Leonel. By evening, when Cesário returned home, Leonel and

Constança had already gotten up. They ate dinner together and waited.

Two comrades showed up, and Cesário introduced them: Manuel and Alberto, who, with others, had reorganized the regional committee. It wasn't necessary for Leonel to introduce himself. They had simply been informed that a comrade sent by the Party Secretariat would be coming to help resolve the present situation.

Manuel was first to speak. Very young, he had a clear, eager voice. The big problem to resolve, he confirmed, was the behavior of comrade Emídio, the present director of reorganization for the regional committee. He always wanted to impose his will. Now he had disappeared, however, since Leonel's arrival had been announced,.

Manuel then described the tasks of each member. Aside from his contact with a nucleus of comrades at the University, who exercised great influence in the Academic Association, he, between biweekly meetings, met regularly with a comrade at the railway station in Figueira da Foz. Alberto met with a nucleus of agricultural workers from Montemor-o-Velho.

"We have no time to lose," Leonel said. "Tomorrow you have to go to Figueira and Montemor-o-Velho and seek out the comrades there to explain the situation."

"I'll take you there," said Cesário. "By car, it's a hop, skip and a jump."

14

They went directly to the house of Fonseca, the railway-man at the Figueira station. That's where Manuel usually met him.

He opened the door himself and faced his visitors with disdain. "What do you want here? I have nothing more to do with you."

"But we have with you, comrade," Manuel answered.

"I have spoken. I want nothing to do with you."

"Can you explain why?"

"Yes. Here goes: You renounced the reorganization. That's it, it's over."

"You're dreaming, comrade. We're all continuing to work. Who put that into your head?"

"The one who had the authority to educate me. The leader of the reorganization, comrade Emídio."

"Aha, it's all clear," Alberto said.

They explained that as soon as he learned that a comrade sent by the Party Secretariat was coming to help resolve the situation Emídio himself had created, he also stopped checking in with the comrade from the Secretariat.

"Impossible!" Fonseca exclaimed.

"It's the truth, friend. Come to the next meeting on the regular day," Cesário told him. "You'll see the situation with your own eyes."

Fonseca looked visibly shocked.

"Don't miss it, comrade," Manuel insisted. "Can we count on you?"

Fonseca hesitated briefly, but accepted their proposal. "I won't miss it."

Their meeting over, Manuel, Alberto and Cesário went to a popular lunchroom to pass some time before continuing on to Montemor-o-Velho. Arriving in the town, they waited another hour past the workday and headed to Carlos's house.

Unlike Fonseca, Carlos received them cordially, although with a certain surprise. "I wasn't expecting to see you here. Emídio told me that you had renounced. I see he deceived me."

"He deceived you and also the comrades from Figueira."

"You know, in the meetings we had, I didn't go along when he wanted to impose his opinions. But I didn't think him capable of such treachery."

"Come to the next meeting, comrade. It's at the usual time and place."

"I'll be there."

15

Everybody showed up. Cesário, Ivone, Leonel and Constança had already dined.

"The issue with Emídio has been resolved," said Leonel. "Unmasked now, he will certainly never turn up again."

Now they had to examine the situation and the reorganization better, as well as the assignments, and how and through whom the liaison with the Party Secretariat would be secured.

Comrades spoke one after another. Emídio's actions, and his provocative lies and intrigues, had successfully led some comrades from Figueira and Montemor-o-Velho to refuse any contact with the comrades in Coimbra and had disrupted all the reorganization work that had begun.

"There was a good chance of enhancing the Party's contact with the railway workers of Alfarelos," said Manuel. "We have to consider how best to pick up this work again."

Here in Coimbra we already have contact with the University and a textile factory, and we're distributing *Avante!* but the rest is completely paralyzed," said Cesário. "Our new tasks will not be easy now."

The other comrades, apart from the Figueira railwayman's hesitations, spoke out in the same manner.

They resolved to retain their former responsibilities. It was only left to decide which comrade would be chosen to secure the liaison with the Party Secretariat.

"I think Cesário is the appropriate comrade," Fonseca unexpectedly rushed to propose. "He's been the most outstanding and capable."

"You're mistaken, Fonseca," said Cesário. "I am not the most appropriate."

"I agree with you, Cesário," Alberto said. "You have performed fundamental work, but for this function, you're not the most appropriate. I propose Manuel."

"I agree," Cesário said.

"I also agree," Carlos backed him up.

"I am sticking to my proposal that it be Cesário," Fonseca insisted.

"And you, Manuel?" Alberto asked. "Cesário, Carlos and I propose you. What do you say?"

Manuel did not respond right away. Was he assessing the new responsibility? Wondering if he would measure up? At last he decided: "I accept."

Thus ended the meeting. Leonel would leave Coimbra right away. Cesário said he would drive them to the old station. The comrades said goodbye and left.

That night, Cesário asked Leonel to wait for the comrade who distributed *Avante!* and who wanted to talk with him. It was Diogo, the same comrade who coordinated Leonel's visit to Coimbra through his distribution network.

The comrade came to the house. He confirmed the departure for the next day and related that they were awaiting his arrival on the freight train to Marinha Grande. He said it was important and they had good news for him.

Constança put on a sour expression.

"It all went well," Leonel said. "And you, Constança?"

She shrugged her shoulders, muttered some unintelligible monosyllable, and gave no more of an answer than that.

"What's going on with you? You're not answering me. Is something going on?"

"Nothing," she responded finally, in a sour mood. "The comrade of the house was good company. She was very nice. But I felt useless. Going on like this, I'm only serving to sleep with you, so...it's over." And she went to bed in a huff.

"Constança!" Leonel insisted. She didn't answer.

Finally, Leonel lay down, in sorrow, and could barely fall asleep.

In the morning when they got up, Constança maintained her guarded, reserved demeanor.

"Did you sleep well?" Leonel asked.

The response was slow in coming: "I slept."

"I don't understand your manners," Leonel murmured. "I understand you're not satisfied, but I don't deserve this." The conversation stopped there.

They packed their clothing bags and Leonel's briefcase. Cesário drove them to the old station. They shared a farewell embrace. "You gave us a lot of help," Cesário said.

The freight train was getting ready to leave. They bought their tickets. For a few minutes, they remained talking on the platform waiting for the passenger compartment car to stop nearby. Constança got on board, and Leonel shared a final embrace with Cesário and jumped onto the car.

The train rolled out, slowly and noisily. One more goodbye from the window and soon the station was far behind, evermore distant.

The train stopped in Marinha Grande. Leonel leaned out the window.

Vasco, along with Marisa, was waiting in the station. They ran to talk with Leonel.

"Big news, comrade. The workers are all stirred up. We're truly heading for a strike. Now, look, here's some more good news."

At Vasco's and Marisa's side, Dog was jumping with joy, facing the rail car and recognizing his master. Leonel stepped down, picked him up and placed him in the compartment under the seat.

"Quiet now, Dog. You know it's forbidden to have you with us."

Dog understood and, licking his master's hands, crouched down obedient and silent.

Vasco shouted, still very happy, "Hey! If you didn't want to keep Dog, we would have kept him. Bye now, we'll be waiting for you tomorrow in Marinha Grande."

The train continued and finally arrived in Cela Nova. It was a morning of radiant sun. Dog accompanied his owners, running, jumping and barking.

Back at the villa house, Constança broke the silence she had kept the whole trip, sleeping or pretending to.

"Come here, Dog," she said, caressing the dog. "You are my only companion here."

Leonel wanted to continue his conversation with Constança.

"You heard, friend. They're predicting there'll be a strike in Marinha Grande. Tomorrow I have to go meet with the comrades before the workday begins in the factories. I'm going to have to leave tonight."

Constança kept her silence for a few moments, then spoke at length.

With such risky work, Leonel could be arrested. What would she do then? If he didn't return, she'd go back to her sisters' house. She couldn't wait there indefinitely for his return.

All this was said in a calm voice, almost indifferently.

"You're right, Constança," Leonel agreed. "You're right. I hope I don't get arrested, and I come back after the strike. But the truth is, it could happen. You're right."

He could leave her enough money for the trip. There wasn't much left, but he'd work that out with the comrades in Marinha Grande. Ending the conversation, Leonel said further, "So, you do know, Constança, I'll be leaving here in the middle of the night."

It took a while for Constança to speak. Then, in a quite unexpected gesture, she approached Leonel and gave him a kiss. "May all go well for you, Leonel."

16

Leonel hopped on his bicycle and rode off in the middle of the night. Constança was sleeping.

Along the way, passing the cement factory, he witnessed an extraordinary sight: Always brightly illuminated by night, it was now completely dark. *A good sign*, Leonel thought. *If everything is dark, it's because they're on strike.*

It was still night when he arrived at Vasco's house. Abel and Tomás were already there. Tomás had no doubts about the outcome: "Victory is certain!" he exclaimed enthusiastically.

"There's still a lot to do," Abel cautioned.

What had to be done has been done, Tomás insisted.

"Well, friends," Leonel said, "the question now is how will we conduct the strike. That's our mission."

Tomás spoke up again. In his view, the local committee, that is, Vasco, Abel and himself, along with Leonel, should remain in permanent session throughout the day. At lunch time, one of them would go out with the Boninés to see what the bosses' response was. He recalled that it had been the Boninés who had personally delivered to the owners of the glass industry the workers' demands that were the basis of the strike.

"Permanent session—how do you mean that?" Abel interrupted. "We all stay here in Vasco's house waiting for events to happen? That's absurd, comrade. Our task is to be alongside the workers, trying to block any strikebreakers, organizing picket lines at factories—and there are some—where there are still doubts about the workers' inclinations."

"Doubts? Where?" Tomás shouted.

"At the windowpane factory, for example," Abel responded.

"Abel's right, Tomás," said Vasco.

Leonel injected his sober voice in contrast to his comrades' excitement. "Abel is completely right. We all have to be at the factory gates organizing picket lines where needed."

With that settled, they distributed tasks. Vasco would swing by the crystal works, where there were many committed comrades also, and check in at other factories with similar conditions, ending up at the front gates of the Roldões factory to watch out for their usual maneuvers to cheat the workers. For example, they could say they were acceding to all the demands just to demobilize the strikers and leave the field free for strikebreakers in the bosses' service, when the only acceptable response to the workers' demands would be given to the Boniné brothers, who had been empowered to negotiate with the bosses at formal sessions.

"So I will go to the windowpane factory. Leave that to me."

"I'll go with you," Leonel decided. "If that's where the biggest problems are, I'll be at your side."

When they arrived, many groups of workers were already waiting for the workday to start.

Next to the factory doors, a brigade from the GNR—*Guarda Nacional Republicana*, the National Republican Guard—were attentively surveilling the workers' movements. In light of the fact that this factory had never seen a strike before, the factory owners were especially concerned that the GNR be there to stop workers from other factories from joining the picket lines.

Abel and Leonel wasted no time: They circulated around to one cluster of workers after another, trying to persuade them not to go in to work.

They had different approaches. Leonel, with his calm, quiet voice, said he worked at Carlos Gallo, and there, as in all the other factories in the glass industry, the strike was total. They should think: If they went to work at the windowpane factory, the bosses in the other factories would use that to open them up to strikebreakers. They listened to Leonel attentively, but few appeared convinced.

Abel worked in another vein entirely, with a loud voice everyone could hear. Sensing some hesitation, he launched his appeal, shouting, "Fellow workmates! In the name of the workers on strike throughout the industry, I call on you, too, in windowpanes: No one go to work!"

Nothing more was required. It was for that, more than anything, that the GNR was waiting to intervene. "Who is this nobody here giving you lessons? We're the ones giving lessons around here."

Quickly their agents seized Abel, unleashing a fury of billy-club blows on his face. They arrested him and, speedily whisking him off, took him prisoner. Leonel ran after to help his comrade, but in the general confusion, the GNR got away.

The workers acted visibly strangely, talking in groups among themselves, discussing what to do next.

Surprise—the GNR intervention had the result opposite than intended. Leonel admiringly watched as the windowpane workers refused to go in to work. The factory closed its doors, and the workers dispersed.

Now Leonel's task was to get Abel released immediately. It was still only eight o'clock in the morning. The local committee comrades had agreed to meet every two hours at Vasco's house to catch up on the strike's progress.

But Leonel couldn't wait until ten and not do anything. He ran to the gates of the crystal factory, and to Carlos Gallo, to see if he could find Vasco so they could decide together what to do.

He managed to find him. Vasco had already gone around to several factories and verified the general work stoppage, and that the workers were sticking together at the gates waiting for the Boninés to appear, announcing that the bosses had given in to the demands.

"Good news and bad news, dear comrade. The windowpane workers are out. But Abel was beaten and taken prisoner."

From the reports coming in, stoppage in all the factories was solid. Now, with the factory doors closed, they had victory happily within sight.

News of the windowpane factory stoppage spread fast, reassuring all the workers that the strike was holding throughout the glass industry. The bosses would be forced to recognize the demands; however, confirmation of this outcome could only be communicated by the Boniné brothers.

Then they would try to mobilize the workforce, in celebration of their victory, to march to the GNR post and demand Abel's immediate release.

At noon, they met again at Vasco's house—he and Tomás. Before long, the Boninés showed up. The bosses, with the general strike and several ovens shut down, had accepted all the demands submitted by the workers.

Now the challenge was to mobilize the entire workforce in all the factories to hail the victory by gathering at the GNR to demand Abel's freedom.

One hour later, workers started gathering there, protesting Abel's detention.

The guardsman at the door stood firmly at his station.

"Bring the sergeant! No delay! Bring the sergeant! No delay!" the crowd shouted.

Afraid that the building might be attacked, the timid, trembling sergeant did come out, arrogant. as always, to disguise his cowardice. "We didn't do him any harm—a few more days in the hole would do him good!" he yelled in a voice that couldn't hide its tremor.

"Not one more day!" shouted someone amongst the demonstrators, immediately picked up by all the others. "Not one more day!"

The sergeant eventually recognized his defeat, but the voice with which he declared himself defeated quavered like his shivering teeth.

"You want this piece of shit? Well, I don't want him here anyway!" And with that, he pushed Abel brutally out into the street.

With one black eye and a bloodied head, Abel, supported by his friends, was carried to the Boninés' pickup. They drove him off, along with Tomás and Vasco.

They headed to Vasco's house for a local cell meeting, with the Boninés and Leonel, and got down to work. Leonel said he'd be back at Vasco's the next day at the close of the workday. They agreed that in the meantime, Vasco would write an article for *Avante!* about the strike, and Leonel another for *The Militant*. They should be finished the next day so that Leonel could submit them for publication.

Losing no more time, Leonel grabbed his bicycle and headed home. Halfway there, the cement factory was all lit up again, and a few hours later, Leonel arrived at the house in the villa.

Constança greeted him with satisfaction and glee. "So, friend? The strike went well?"

In a few words, Leonel reported on the huge victory.

"You know something?" Constança said. "We agreed I'd wait for you two or three days before going back to my sisters, but I was prepared to wait a whole week for you."

To Leonel's surprise, when he told her he'd be returning to Marinha Grande the next day, she said nothing.

17

They spent the morning in the usual manner: wash, breakfast, the door open, and Dog with one paw on the sill waiting for them to invite him in and give him something to eat. They enjoyed the gallantry of his entrance and his meal, and his licking the plate.

After a few hours in the open air, and then lunch, Leonel mounted his bicycle and in no special hurry made his way to arrive at Vasco's house at the end of the workday. He was punctual, and while they waited for the other comrades, Vasco read his article about the strike that he wrote for *Avante!*

"Is it good?"

"It's very good," Leonel said. "But I think it would be helpful if you added two or three ideas."

"Such as?"

"You'd want to refer to three decisive factors for victory. One was the existence of a leadership profoundly knowledgeable about the situation. Another was the contact with the masses of workers and the intimate, objective familiarity with their spirit and their resistance. And finally, the permanent, ongoing work of clarifying the issues. What do you think?"

"Yes, I agree. I've taken note. Before the comrades arrive, I'll edit it quickly so you can take the original to *Avante!*"

Shortly after, Tomás and Abel arrived, the latter with a black eye and head covered with fresh wounds from his beating.

Before the meeting began, Tomás said he wanted to discuss a previous question.

Great, Vasco thought, *there goes Tomás with all his hesitations*. But it was exactly to the contrary.

Tomás recalled that, on the morning of the strike, he had suggested that the local cell members stay at Vasco's house in permanent session. He wanted to acknowledge that Abel was perfectly right in getting them out to the factories and thus guaranteeing the participation of the whole glass industry in the strike.

"It's positive that you felt the need to come and acknowledge that in this first meeting the day after the strike," Leonel remarked.

Vasco began by informing Leonel of some important events that occurred later that day of the strike after he had returned home.

News of the victorious strike traveled rapidly throughout the region. To commemorate the occasion, comrades from the Tomé Feteira File Factory in Vieira de Leiria came to Marinha Grande, and from the cement factory and from the Nazaré. By nighttime, they were joined by others from the tableware factory in Alcobaça. They all brought excellent reports of the growth of the organization and the struggles in progress.

At the following local committee meeting that they held, they took certain measures.

"You can report, Abel," Vasco proposed.

Abel detailed several important decisions they had made and hoped Leonel would support them: Maintain the local committee with the same composition, Vasco, Abel and Tomás. Create a Coordinating Commission for regional work with the following composition: Vasco, comrade Silvino from the Tomé Feteira File Factory and comrade José from cement. Vasco would secure the contact with other entities that would join later.

The meeting ended. They set the next one, with Leonel, in two weeks' time. In a spirit of deep satisfaction, they said goodnight, and Leonel returned home on his bicycle.

18

Constança watched him come in and made no comment. Even when Leonel told her he wouldn't be leaving the house for a full two weeks, she said nothing.

"Look," Leonel said, "I'm going to take advantage of this time to write an article for *The Militant*, and read and study a work of Lenin that interests me a great deal."

Days later, according to plan, Valdo came to the house at the villa. The first question he asked was completely unanticipated. "Listen, do you know how to drive a car? I have the impression you once told me you do."

Leonel confirmed that, when he was quite young, he had worked in an auto shop, learned to drive and even took out a driver's license.

So Valdo went directly to the main point that brought him there: Alexandre, a comrade and former member of the Secretariat who had been kept prisoner for many years at the Fort of Angra do Heroismo in the Azores, had been relocated to the continent and was now interned at the Prison Hospital at Caxias. The pretext was violent pain brought on by a supernumerary tooth that had grown into the roots of his other teeth. In fact, he didn't hurt. But the critical thing is that he was thinking, and already had a plan, of escaping from prison.

The two comrades took special care not to be heard, which did not escape Constança's observation when, the few times she entered the main room, they suddenly went quiet.

"Listen, Leonel, if you're planning some new project, don't count on me. If we leave this house, I'll go back to living with my sisters. I'd love to take Dog, but I won't have the right circumstances for it."

That night, in bed, Leonel asked, "So, Constança? As you know, I love you very much—"

The response was calm and unemotional: "I don't feel the same way, Leonel. I loved you, I left my sisters' house, I stayed with you when you went underground, but as a man, today, I'm completely indifferent about you."

19

They had to let Dona Maria Pedrosa know they were going away from Cela Velha. They sought her out in her residence, accompanied by Dog. She received them in her salon. Leonel told her he had gotten well-paying work in a distant region and for that reason, they had to leave.

On receiving the news, Dona Maria exclaimed, "I won't accept the months you paid in advance."

Her visitors assured her they weren't interested in being repaid any money. Dona Maria thought a little:

"I know you didn't bring kitchen things—pots and pans. The house at the villa had all that, but you can't go away without those necessities. The things there were my brother's and I'm not offering them. They're a reminder of him that I'd like to keep. But tomorrow I'll tell my caretaker to go to Alcobaça and buy you a set a pots and pans that I can offer you."

Before saying goodbye, she added, "I consider you real friends. If at any time you pass through Cela Velha again, pay me a visit. It would be a great pleasure for me."

Visibly moved, she rose and started to walk with them to the door. Outside, the boys she was raising were cavorting happily with Dog. Leonel and Constança, with Dog excitedly jumping around their feet, said farewell, kissing the children affectionately, and withdrew to their house.

Turning backward, they saw what they had seen on one other occasion: Dona Maria and the boys waving them goodbye.

20

There was news in Marinha Grande. Tomás's neighbor Rui had issued him a challenge the day of the strike: "Listen, Tomás! Isn't it too much work for you to take on the printing of the strike communiqués? You don't have to deny it—I can hear it perfectly. I propose that I take over this job. You'll preserve your energy, and I assure you I will do it in good faith."

Tomás agreed. But following the police action, they discovered that Rui was the printer, and they took him to Lisbon. He managed to communicate through the comrades in the Aljube prison that he had been violently beaten, but he assured them that he had not—and would not say—anything, whatever the cops did to him.

21

A few days later, Valdo returned to the house at the villa. He had a new task for Leonel with a high level of responsibility. It was about setting up a clandestine house.

"You and Constança set yourselves up in that house. Comrade Alexandre will be brought there by automobile, to be protected there after his escape from the Hospital in Caxias."

"Don't count on Constança. She's going to her sisters' house as soon as we vacate this one."

"Well, then, another woman—a comrade—will go with you," Valdo answered.

Valdo reported that he had decided to establish direct contact with Vasco, who, in Leonel's place, was showing himself to be entirely capable of leading the regional organization, now much bigger than before.

22

Things proceeded rapidly. Valdo gave Leonel a car and told him to find a house in the area of Mafra and Ericeira. Leonel lost no time. In the designated area, he discovered, outside the town of Achada, on an uninhabited stretch of the road, a house in the middle of a garden that had in its windows the usual signs about the place being for rent. The name of the owner was given—Horácio—who could be found at the Central grocery store in Mafra. Leonel went to see him.

The owner was in a hurry to rent the house and the deal was sealed. The façade had one distinguishing feature: painted in black, against a white background, a large number of little birds. Thus the name by which it was known: the Estate of the Little Birds.

23

Preparation for Alexandre's escape went quickly and carefully.

The prison at Caxias was not equipped to deal with the urgency of his violent pains at the root of one of his teeth, which he insisted required a prompt extraction. So the police transported him to the Hospital of Santa Marta. It was a complicated case, and they brought him there several times. They led him to the door of the stomatology department and waited to take him back to Caxias.

Alexandre noticed that while he entered the clinic and the police waited for him, many of the patients, done with their treatment, exited by a door in the back. Advised of this, his comrades verified how things worked in the hospital and confirmed that leaving by that other door and passing through several corridors, one could reach the hospital front gate.

On the appointed date, Alexandre followed that route, and at the hospital door, Leonel, with a woman, was waiting in a car whose license plate number had been provided to Alexandre.

They headed straight to the Estate of the Little Birds. Leonel opened the gate, drove the car into the garden and returned to close the gate. Dog, who had moved along with his master, ran to welcome them.

They talked for a while in the dining room and got to know one another.

The woman, who called herself Ruth, said she had been dispatched from an underground printshop where the comrades were capable of continuing their work without her.

Leonel spoke of his life as a militant, but in few words.

24

For some time, all went according to expectation at the Estate of the Little Birds.

Leonel drove Alexandre to meetings of the Secretariat, which he had rejoined, and picked him up after nightfall.

Ruth stayed at home, alert to anything unusual that might occur.

In the garden, Dog played with his usual boisterousness.

One day, however, strange things happened. Coming from Mafra and past the town of Achada, Leonel saw an unfamiliar figure wandering in the road on a stretch where the first house was the Estate of the Little Birds. It was a woman, but of a suspect size and gait, her face almost concealed by a shawl, her step quite long, and a walk altogether too accelerated for an almost deserted road.

Immediately returning home, Leonel put the car in the garden and waited. It didn't take long: The strange figure came and approached the gate.

"Quick!" he said to Ruth. "Go see what she wants." Ruth went to the gate just as the strange person placed a hand on the bolt.

"What do you want?" Ruth shouted.

"I just wanted to see the house" came the response in the unmistakable tones of a man. Having said which, he turned around and walked back in the direction of Achada.

Driving his car fast toward Mafra, Leonel saw the man in disguise almost running toward Achada.

The comrades took immediate action. Into the car they went, with papers, books and all the other political material, and Dog.

After closing the gate to his Estate, Leonel immediately sped out to the place where he customarily drove Alexandre.

He dropped Ruth and Dog off in a park, and shortly the Secretariat took measures: Alexandre stayed at the Secretariat locale, and they arranged for Leonel and Ruth to stay for a few days at some other comrades' house.

25

Leonel, accompanied by Ruth, was chosen to direct a large Party organization far away. They rented a house with a little garden, where Dog played his part with his masters in his usual way.

The organization progressed, the number of members grew, they went through great mass struggles. The Party advanced successfully.

One day, out of the blue, Valdo, on a visit to the region, showed up at their house. He used the occasion to talk with them—precisely with them and not with others, considering all he knew about them, and their deep understanding of the realities. He quickly got to the point. Since Leonel had left his home for the underground, until the present moment, only a few months had passed. And he, Valdo, thought a lot about the future.

The struggle would still be long and hard. There would be memorable victories—and defeats. Many comrades would pay for their dedication to the struggle with long years in prison, torture by the police, even with their lives, murdered by fascism. But surely, surely, the great day would come eventually. The fascist dictatorship would be overturned, freedom would be won, and the Party would emerge as a transformative revolutionary force.

"So that's what I wanted to share with you, my beloved comrades, the certainty I feel about the future of our Party and our people."

The Vargas Case:
Death of a Landowner

TÓ-ZÉ, Santarém's son, had gone bird hunting in the pine forest of the village.

He found himself deep in the woods tracking a blackbird when he glanced out into the distance, where clusters of low bushes cut across the horizon. From there he saw, somewhat indistinctly, the blur of the modest roadway toward the Manor.

That's when Tó-Zé froze in astonishment. Sprawled on the ground piled with pine needles, a man appeared to be sleeping. The boy couldn't resist temptation and drew closer to get a better look.

His curiosity turned to shock and fear when the man gave no signs of life. It was none other than Vargas, the rich landowner of the Manor.

Tó-Zé ran to the settlement. "Vargas is dead in the pine forest," he shouted to everyone he passed as he continued running.

"Are you making up stories? Stop with your idiotic jokes," people replied. No one took him seriously. He arrived home and called for his father.

"Did you have a good look?"

"Yes, I saw him very well. It's him."

And the two of them took off. Now it was Santarém shouting, "Vargas is dead! In the pine forest!" But as he was well-known as a joker and trickster, only his neighbor José Afonso, and his brother, lame João, followed after them. Led by Tó-Zé, they arrived at the spot.

There was no doubt. It certainly was Vargas, chest up, his arms crossed, his shirt splattered with blood.

Some fifty meters away, parked on the side of the road, with the headlights on low beam, sat Vargas's unmistakable yellow car. Obviously, he had left it there before entering the forest, where he was killed.

They circled around the body. Only lame João acted somewhat strangely. He bent down and, unnoticed, picked up something from the ground that he placed in his pocket. Then he and his brother returned to the village.

Meanwhile, the people's curiosity aroused, dozens of villagers wound up gathering at the crime scene.

Above the collective silence Santarém's strong voice rose up. "Boys! We have to carry the guy back to the Manor!" And as everyone kept their silence, he shouted, "Tó-Zé! Go to the village and find a stretcher! Someone will help you carry it."

It took a while, but Tó-Zé finally brought the stretcher with the help of Matias the carpenter, whom he encountered and urged to come with him. They threw the dead body on the stretcher as if it were a sack of potatoes.

"Will you come with me to take him away?" Santarém asked Matias the carpenter.

Yes, why not? And the two secured their fists on the stretcher and got ready to move.

At that moment, alerted by the news and with his bicycle in hand, the nervous sergeant of the National Guard of the Republic—the GNR—showed up. He saw the stretcher with the body and quickly looked around. "What's going on? Are you crazy or what? Who was the first person to move the body? Huh?" Greeted with silence, he continued, "No one should have touched him before the Health Department got here. Didn't you know that? Now put him down gently."

Without taking his hands off the stretcher, Santarém responded, "That's a great idea, Sergeant. A week from now he'd still be here rotting away feeding the flies."

"You don't know what you're talking about," the sergeant snapped. "Don't you see you're erasing all the evidence of the crime?"

The ground was all a trampled mess. The sergeant was right, but Santarém made out as though he hadn't heard. "Let's go," he said, and took a step forward.

"Halt!" the sergeant cried, his hand cradling the handle of his pistol, but his voice sounded weak and without conviction.

Santarém and Matias the carpenter set the stretcher down. "How are you going to stop us? Kill us?" Santarém asked and laughed. And sensing the sergeant's hesitation, he yelled, "Matias, hold on tight. We're taking him to the Manor."

They waited no longer. And despite the terrified astonishment of the crowd, the two proceeded with the litter, with Tó-Zé alongside his father. No one accompanied them.

The sergeant suddenly changed his attitude. "At the end of the day, maybe they're right," he murmured. "Who knows when the Health Department would have gotten here. There was no way we could just leave the body rotting there." Then, at the last-minute, he shouted out to them as they departed. "Hey! Tell them to come get the car. Because if it's left here, someone will steal it."

Then he turned toward the crowd, commenting, "They're going to pay dearly for this joke. But what can we do?"

One after another, people in the crowd started leaving. The scene soon became deserted and still, as if only the horrible memory of the crime remained behind, filling the space.

Now with the place void of people, Pinto the coalman appeared, as though he had been waiting for everyone to leave before he ventured forward.

He stopped, looked at the ground, glanced all around and hurried away, turning to one side and the other, perhaps afraid someone might have seen him.

Meanwhile, Santarém and Matias the carpenter continued their march. The Manor was still a ways off. They paused from time to time to rest, placing the stretcher on the ground.

"Whew!" Santarém huffed. "Was this guy made of lead?"

Matias the carpenter said nothing. Skinny and sinewy, he remained standing erect.

Tó-Zé picked up stones lying on the road and hurled them, measuring the distance of each throw.

In time, they arrived at the Manor. A servant, barely able to hold back a large, powerful dog that was barking threateningly, asked why they had come, and on learning the reason, horrified, he opened the gate and let them enter.

They crossed the wide, paved courtyard directly to the house. Inside, they were received by Dona Alzira, to whom the deceased was married.

While the numerous household staff took the stretcher away to another room, which they then closed off, everyone cried—or pretended to cry—over the death of their master. Dona Alzira, cold and contained, cried, too, but, more than lamenting the dead man, she seemed determined from the very start to point out who the killers were. "I know very well who killed him!" she burst out repeatedly. "I know for sure, without any doubt!"

* * *

No one from the Health Department ever showed up. The funeral took place, but the family did not call upon a priest to officiate.

Arriving from long distances in their cars, several close relatives came to the Manor, all in dark clothes and black ties. The mortuary workers had washed and dressed the body professionally, arranged him in the coffin, which they had previously delivered, and placed the coffin in the hearse. There was no wreath, no sash, not even a flower.

The small, sad cortege passed through the street on the way to the town cemetery. Only Tó-Zé ran to watch it go by.

A week later, Sanches, from the Judiciary Police, arrived in an old car. Short and skinny, and carelessly dressed, it was no wonder, when he learned about the funeral, that he expressed his shock.

"If he was killed by gunshot, they didn't even retrieve the bullets from his body, and disinterring him now for an autopsy would not be easy."

The sergeant took him to the scene of the crime. "This is where they found him," he pointed.

Sanches looked, took a few steps around the vicinity and stopped. "Everything has been disturbed, seemingly on purpose," he concluded, turning his focus on the spot where the body was discovered. "They wiped out all evidence of the crime. This investigation has a bad beginning."

After a few reflective minutes, he offered, "Now we have to uncover who would have had a motive that would lead them to kill him."

The sergeant gave him a few starting points. He explained how he had arrived at the spot, and recalled the people who were there at the time. Santarém, Matias the carpenter and many others.

Santarém stood out in particular. He was the one who argued for the immediate removal of the body and had responded to the sergeant so provocatively—not a normal response.

According to what people told him, José Afonso had arrived at the scene, looked about and retreated. "If he went there right away and returned home right away, that's also not normal, don't you think?" Sanches observed. "We could begin with either of these two."

"One more question," the sergeant continued. He also knew, from what the staff at the Manor told him, that when the stretcher came with the dead body, the lady asserted, repeatedly, that she was certain who had killed him.

"Good," Sanches announced. "Then first I'll go and talk with the widow." So the sergeant brought him to the Manor.

Sanches declared his identity and was received in a hall of upholstered chairs where, shortly, walking at an exaggeratedly slow pace, Dona Alzira appeared. She seated herself and, before the police agent could speak, said in a deliberate, imposing manner, "What do you want now? Can you bring my husband back to life? Leave me in peace!"

"Just one question," Sanches stated.

"I have nothing more to add. Nothing! Absolutely nothing!"

"I've heard that you claimed you knew who the killer was. Is it true you said that?"

"And so what if I said it? I already see it didn't get us anywhere. What can you do here?"

Her explosive prickliness riled Sanches. "You're completely right. But did you or did you not say you knew who the criminal was?" His calm had turned to irritation and now to anger. "Did you say it or not?"

"Yes, I said it, it's true. I know very well who killed him."

"Who?"

She answered instantly. "José Afonso. It couldn't have been anyone else."

"Thank you very much." Sanches made a little bow and left.

"Listen!" Dona Alzira called out. Sanches didn't respond.

The sergeant was waiting for him at the Manor gate. "The lady says the killer is José Afonso. You already told me he was at the scene. Do you know anything else about him? Do you know him well?"

"Yes, he was at the scene. But as I told you, he left right away. Would you like me to take you to his house?"

"We'll talk to him later. Let's start with Santarém."

* * *

They found him in his modest house with its front door facing the street. The lands he rented from Vargas were elsewhere. Santarém himself opened the door. It looked like he was expecting them.

The sergeant had no need to explain who the other man was who accompanied him.

"Come in, come in, Senhor Judiciary. I'll be very happy to talk with you." It sounded like an insolent wisecrack. They sat down. Santarém's wife Clotilde hurried in to listen to the interrogation.

"There are two things I'd like you to explain," Sanches began. "Why did you go to the scene of the crime so early in the morning, and then so quickly move the cadaver to the Manor?"

"I went there because it's my son who discovered the cadaver and ran to tell me. And, as I said at the time to the sergeant here, I took the body to the Manor so it wouldn't stay there and rot until the Health Department people finally showed up. And now, you answer me, would it have been better if the body was still there?"

"Just one more question," said Sanches, irritated by the response. "Where were you the night of Thursday, the 12th?"

"Beautiful question," Santarém laughed ironically. "I don't remember. Let me see. It was more than a week ago. No, I can't recall."

"You don't recall?"

"No. No, I don't recall."

"It would be better if you did recall."

"Maybe it would, but I don't remember, what can you do?"

Tó-Zé sat in on the interrogation, his eyes shining. He was clearly enjoying his father's answers.

Clotilde, sitting a little farther back, showed visible signs of displeasure.

"We'll leave it at that for today. But we'll see you again. Until then," said Sanches as he took his leave.

After Sanches had left, it was Clotilde's turn to interrogate her husband. She truly did not understand him. Neither the story of having taken the body away on a stretcher, nor that silly response about not recalling where he had been the night of the crime. He was at home, she recalled perfectly. Why did he make such a scene?

Arrogant as he had been toward the police, Santarém showed himself sensitive to his wife. He was just that way, as she well knew. If he had taken the corpse to the Manor, he had his reasons.

"Reasons? What reasons? The other time you had your reasons and look at what happened."

She had been left alone for a year with her son, enduring so many hardships that she was tempted to kill herself. And all because of what he did, and on account of his character. What did he want? For that situation to repeat itself? She couldn't bear it. And she started to cry.

Santarém then pronounced enigmatically: "Relax. The police will never discover it."

"Discover what?" Clotilde shouted, but he had already turned away.

* * *

"Let's go to this José Afonso's home now," Sanches decided.

The courtyard had a chicken coop and rabbit hutch, a well, a properly tended vegetable garden, and a barking dog.

"Quiet, Sultan!" a fresh feminine voice was heard. Shortly a lovely young woman came into view.

"It's Gabriela," the sergeant whispered. "I'll tell you the story later."

"Wait here, I'll go call my father."

José Afonso didn't hurry. When he appeared, he was alone.

"I wonder, Senhor José Afonso, they told me you have a whole bunch of kids and I only see this girl."

"They're all doing their chores in the fields. They're the ones who support us here."

"Senhor José," Sanches continued after identifying himself, "just one question. Why were you among the first who went to the scene of the crime and then turned around and left?"

Calmly he answered, "To see if they had truly found Vargas dead. Just that."

"To see if he was really dead?"

"Not to see if Vargas was dead, but to see if it was Vargas."

"Very well," Sanches continued, admiring the cleverness of the response. "And where were you the previous night?"

José Afonso appeared to hesitate. "I remember it well," he said finally. "I was at Ernesto's tavern having a drink or two."

Sanches noticed the hesitation. "We'll go see—"

"Go ahead," José Afonso interrupted calmly.

"We'll go see," Sanches said again. And he left with no further conversation.

"This man has real self-control: he measures every word he says," he observed outside. He turned toward the sergeant. "When we were about to leave the house, a lame guy with a lot of difficulty walking entered. Do you know who that is?"

"Yes, I do. That's João, José Afonso's brother."

"Quick, go back in and tell him to come out here."

"He's just a poor devil," the sergeant said. "He wouldn't hurt a fly. He was also one of the first ones to arrive after they found the body. But he didn't stick around and he left with his brother. Poor devil."

"Take note, Sergeant," Sanches observed. "In an investigation there aren't poor devils and suspects. Everybody could be a suspect. Go on, go get him out here." The sergeant brought him out.

"Listen, Senhor João," Sanches began, "I'd like to ask you a few little questions."

"Ask, ask—"

"You were at the crime scene right after the body was discovered. For what reason?"

"I might not have gone, but Santarém called my brother and I followed them to see."

"And tell me, what did you feel when you saw the dead body?"

"I was taken aback. But also I figured he treated the people so badly that there must have been a lot of people who wished him ill."

"Do you mean, you thought it was good they killed him?"

"I didn't say that, Senhor Agent. We can't have a worthwhile conversation that way."

"All right. And where were you the night of the crime?"

The response came out with unflappable calm. "At home. You can go ask." And he added with an edge, "If you go there, you'll see that José has so many children that I won't lack for witnesses."

"Very well, for today. See you again, Senhor João."

"See you again. Be well."

A few paces from the house, Sanches turned to the sergeant. "He is hardly some poor devil! He's like his brother, measuring every word that comes out of his mouth.

* * *

It was apparent that Sanches was not satisfied. "Listen, Sergeant, you told me that this Matias the carpenter helped carry the stretcher with the body. But you haven't told me anything more about him."

No, it didn't seem necessary, so far as the sergeant knew or suspected. Matias the carpenter had nothing to do with Vargas, nor any reason to wish him harm.

"How do you know? And the others? Did they have reason?" Sanches pressed.

"To kill him, no. But to wish him harm, yes." As for Matias the carpenter, his life was transparent. Every day he rode his bicycle to town, he earned decent money, and worked the whole day. But, agreeing with Sanches, it would be good to interrogate him.

That Saturday they knocked on his door. A woman opened it, direct and friendly. She told them to come into a modest little parlor smelling of wildflowers. Very soon her husband entered.

"I'm Agent Sanches from the Judiciary Police. I'd like it if you could shed some light on a few questions."

"Go ahead."

"You were one of the first to show up at the spot where they found Vargas dead. You and Santarém carried the stretcher with the body to the Manor. Can you explain how this happened?"

"Naturally," Matias responded. "I went there because a young kid came from there asking me to bring a stretcher. And I helped lift the stretcher with the body because Santarém couldn't do it by himself."

"That doesn't explain anything," Sanches said. And he proceeded to bombard Matias with further questions.

Matias answered them all. Where he worked, how much he earned, where he spent his time.

"And nights you go to the tavern?"

"I've never set foot in it. I stay at home with my wife and sometimes read a magazine or a book—"

"You read?" Sanches was amazed.

"Yes, I read. And just so you don't pester me with more questions, I want to say that I don't have lands, I owe nothing to anyone, and I never had anything personal against Vargas."

"Meaning," Sanches remarked before leaving the house, "you mixed yourself up in this mess without even knowing why."

"If that's the way you see it," Matias replied.

Outside, Sanches told the sergeant, "Dangerous man, my friend. And you said his life was transparent."

"I d-don't understand," the sergeant stammered.

"Don't you see? Here in a village like this a man who reads books and magazines? Dangerous, better believe it."

* * *

José Afonso had said he had spent the night of the crime at the tavern knocking back a drink or two. It would be well to verify that.

The sergeant showed him where the tavern was, and Sanches went in by himself. The large saloon was packed, some standing, some seated, all drinking. Given that the village was but a settlement of small landholders, it was evident that nighttimes, everyone headed to the bar.

Sanches made for the counter. People let him through begrudgingly, with untrusting, hostile glares. As soon as Sanches reached the counter, Pinto the coalman stole out to the street—a bad sign.

The only person who welcomed him cordially was Ernesto the tavernkeep, a tall, nonchalant man with red hair. Sanches started up a conversation.

"Your place is always like this with so many people?"

"Always."

"Do you know them all?"

"Certainly, I do. Like the back of my hand."

"Listen, can you tell me if a certain José Afonso is here?"

The barkeep looked all around deviously, but clearly wasn't searching for anybody. "No, I'm not seeing him here today."

"Good. I need some information and I'm going to ask you. Do you recall if he was here the night before they found Vargas dead?"

The taverner did not seem surprised by the question. "I see you're from the police. So I will answer you in good faith because I want the killer to be discovered the sooner the better." He paused a few moments, then continued. "You know what? It's been quite a few days now but everyone around here is still thinking about these things. Who might it have been, and who it definitely wasn't. I myself think about this one and that one, with a lot of doubts—"

"Everything you're saying is very interesting," Sanches interrupted. "But you didn't answer my question. Was José Afonso here or not?"

"Why shouldn't I respond? With absolute certainty, he was here that night."

"With absolute certainty?"

"Yes, with absolute certainty."

"There's always such a big crowd here, and it's already some days ago now, yet you are so certain? Your memory is impressive."

"Happily, I can't complain about it."

"With such a good memory, and people coming here every night, you really know them all?"

"Yes, without exception."

"And what do you know about them?"

"I know who they are, what they do, their family stories. Like the back of my hand, as I just told you."

"So, since you've been thinking so much about the crime, do you suspect anyone?"

The barkeep didn't answer right away. "You know, we're all suspects here—"

"Nice response, Senhor Ernesto. And have you been to the crime scene yet?"

"No, never."

"Not the morning they found Vargas, nor later?"

"Not that morning, nor before, nor after."

"How can you state you've never gone there if you don't know where it is?" Sanches smiled proudly at the acumen of his own question. And, excited by a sudden and crazy inspiration, he presented an idea that he deemed brilliant. "We can verify if you did or did not set foot there. Can you show me the soles of your boots?"

"If I understand you correctly, your idea is very funny. If you're going to suspect anyone with pine needles on their soles, no one from around here is going to be innocent."

"Very well." Sanches, incensed by that response, insisted, "Show me the soles of your boots."

The customers that night then witnessed an unimaginable scene—Sanches walking behind the counter, and Ernesto lifting each leg to show him the soles of his boots.

"Curious," a confused Sanches mumbled. "Not one pine needle. Not even a little piece of one, almost as if you had washed them off."

"The ground here is always wet," Ernesto explained so solemnly that it was apparent he was now mocking him.

Sanches left in a foul mood. When he had first arrived, he thought he would interrogate a few of those present. After that scene, there was nothing more to do but get out, and fast. On the way out, some barely disguised their laughter, others turned their backs, while still others stood rigidly staring him in the face almost in defiance. He gave up.

The next day, Sanches went to the Guard post in the town. From the village, people arrived to attend Sunday mass, and also to visit the market and the grocery shops.

He told the chief at the post that he was suspending his investigation and would make a report to the Judiciary central office. Later he—or someone else—would take up this case again.

Questioning the presumed suspects had aroused more doubts and suspicions than it had offered clarity or leads. The more explicit the answers, the more doubts they raised. From what people said under interrogation, it seemed everyone wanted to be considered a suspect. He had to go to Central to decide how to proceed.

* * *

Before retiring from the case, Sanches decided, by some inexplicable intuition, to pass by the Manor and say goodbye to the widow. Dona Alzira, standing and frowning, received him. Sanches got down to business.

"Do you still maintain the accusation you ma—"

"I've already told you to leave me alone, do you hear?" Dona Alzira interrupted him. "Or would you prefer that my servants put you outside?"

"Do you maintain it or not?"

Dona Alzira lost control in a sudden change of attitude. "Sit down!" she shouted. "If you want to know why I maintain it, hear me without interrupting." And speaking rapidly, turning hoarse with rage, she launched into not so much an explanation as an act of denunciation.

Responsibility for the crime and for everything that happened lay with Gabriela, José Afonso's daughter. She herself, the mistress of the house, had welcomed her in, gave her work as a housemaid, and looked after her almost as if she were her own daughter. It was truly a work of charity on her part, because she well knew about José Afonso's passel of kids, and employing the daughter alleviated some of the family's burden. And here's the thanks I got: Gabriela got herself involved with my husband and, when she returned home, her father accused Vargas of abusing his daughter. And on top of that, he invented this story that the lord of the Manor intended to take away from him, with no explanation, the best lands he rented out.

"It was he who killed him, without any doubt!" she concluded, fuming.

"This is beginning to get interesting," Sanches murmured. And he kept to his decision to go to Central to see how he should proceed.

In the village, little was said about Gabriela's situation. They lamented her bad fortune, and held her as Vargas's victim. Nor was she the first. There was much talk about her case. Most memorable had been a comment by Santarém: "If she'd been a daughter of mine, I would gladly have cleaned his clock!"

* * *

Dressed in dark clothes, but with bright headscarves, the Gertrudes sisters, two old ladies who gladly spoke ill of everyone, ran around excitedly ever since the death of Vargas. The news came to them, but they knew nothing more.

They saw Sanches in his old car, the GNR sergeant on his bicycle, now apart and now standing together, but they didn't find out what they were planning to do.

They didn't live near the houses where the officials interrogated the suspects, nor did they have the legs to follow them around.

Without access to verifiable news, they set about inventing it between themselves, to spread through the village. "Ay, sister," one said, "there they go. Where would they be going?"

"The hurry they're in, they must be about to arrest someone," said the other.

One time, when Pinto the coalman passed by them almost at a run, one of them commented, "He's escaping."

And the other added, "He must have robbed someone."

So they put out the word that Pinto the coalman had committed some crime.

Everybody laughed. They knew Pinto well, with his own strange way of walking and his mysterious crane-like aloofness.

The Gertrudes sisters thus went around rattling their brains with stories, but not sufficiently to take on any traction in the village.

Until one day, in a most unexpected way, they finally found a subject, and a big one at that, they could gossip about in their special way.

Sundays, they usually went to mass in town and stayed talking with some of the old ladies who sought, in their animated conversations, some reason to maintain an interest in life.

And right there in the public square an unimaginable encounter awaited them. Ernesto the tavernkeep, with his red hair rustling in the air, headed straight for them.

"So, aunties, have you heard the latest?"

They adjusted their kerchiefs and leaned in. Ernesto fired off, "They know who killed Vargas." And having aroused the old ladies' avid curiosity, he told them the whole sordid tale, which he knew perfectly. A worker from the Manor went to have a few drinks at the tavern and revealed everything. Dona Alzira shouted it out good and loud that the killer was José Afonso. And she did not merely accuse him. She gave proof it was him. "Proven proofs," Ernesto emphasized.

The old ladies listened with rapt attention. Their mouths hanging open, they uttered exclamations as Ernesto told the story. "Oh... Ah! ... I thought so... the beast... you don't say... Ah!... Oh!..."

Ernesto knew very well what would happen. The next day everyone in town would know about Dona Alzira's accusation. And despite the fact that the Gertrudes sisters were well known for their malicious talk, some of it would stay floating in the air.

As the news spread, as could be expected, it reached the ears of Matias the carpenter. He went to speak with José Afonso. "Let them talk," is all José said.

Matias the carpenter did not feel satisfied dropping the conversation like that. "The most important thing," he said, "is why Ernesto set that news in motion. What does he want? Really? To offer you up to the whole town, as the already proven one who committed the crime?"

"That much is clear," said José Afonso, "but what remains to be known is why he's doing that."

* * *

The story the worker from the Manor told at the bar about what happened there traveled from mouth to mouth.

Before the crime, the one giving orders was naturally Vargas. But it was Brites, an employee at the house, who carried them out. This was not simply hearsay: It was confirmed by the farm workers renting land from the Manor, as well as those employed at the Manor.

One of the workers recounted that it was Brites who hired him, and also who fired him. Another remembered that, forcing payment on a debt, it was Brites who threatened him with taking his lands away. Someone else, that Brites kept the accounts with him and paid his wages. Many others, too, said it was Brites who always showed up to collect the rent.

In conclusion, as much as Vargas, Brites himself deserved the ill will of the whole village.

At the bar, Pinto the coalman, generally one of few words, came out with an explosive comment. "If there were motives to kill Vargas, there were also motives to get rid of Brites."

"That's going too far, Pinto," said someone alongside him. "Who knows what someone might think if they heard you say that?"

Regretting having spoken, Pinto left right away in a hurry.

With Vargas dead, Dona Alzira, shouting at everyone for no reason, showed herself completely incapable of assuming direction of the estate. Predictably, one day one of those relatives who had shown up at the funeral in their dark suit and black tie would appear to take over from Vargas. And Brites would continue to serve as that person's flunky.

Vargas had been a voracious landowner who exploited, threatened and persecuted the small farmers and the poor who asked him for money loans. Whoever replaced him wouldn't be much different.

In the end, it was not just Vargas. It was the estate, and the wealth of the Manor, its owners and its loyal hired staff, that was the source of the poor existence, the problems, the dramas, the anxieties of the people in the village. Vargas was dead. But the Manor, and all that wealth invested across a dispersed settlement of destitute people, would continue its dominating, aggressively exploitative presence.

* * *

José Afonso began noticing that his brother had started leaving the house well before dawn and stayed away several hours before returning. Where was he going? And doing what? This had only begun recently.

"Do any of you know where João is going?" he asked his children. "Or what he's doing?"

No, no one knew.

José Afonso called upon his eldest son. "Get up early, and follow your uncle so he doesn't see you, and find out where he's going and what he's doing."

Joaquim complied with his father's instructions.

João crossed the settlement of houses and followed a series of paths heading toward the pine forest. Every once in a while, he stopped, turned around and looked around for a few moments. Joaquim managed not to be seen. He had never followed anyone before, but he showed a special aptitude for the task.

João entered the pine forest, walked a good stretch farther, halted in a clearing and sat down to rest.

What place was this? What had he come here to do? Joaquim chose a spot where he could not be seen and waited patiently.

After a while, João rose and started walking back and forth in curious patterns. Ten or fifteen steps in one direction, then the same in the other direction. Always bent over the ground, mixing up the pine needles with a stick. Once, twice, three times, innumerable times, in different directions. Then he sat leaning against a pine tree. He seemed to have fallen asleep, breathing in deeply the fresh, fragrant aroma of the resin.

Finally, he stretched his limbs, got up and went back to the ground, bending over it and stirring up the low-growing plants.

Joaquim started getting tired and bored. He was just at the point of not waiting for his uncle any longer when João suddenly stopped and took off on the return route. Joaquim made a quick shortcut through familiar roads and trails and arrived home in no time.

"So?" his father asked. He recounted what he saw. Describing the site they had gone to, José Afonso said, "How strange. That's where Vargas was found dead."

He waited. In time, his brother arrived. "A long walk," José Afonso said. "Where did you go?"

João smiled and, holding his arm out, showed a bouquet of wildflowers that he picked for his nieces.

As José started to leave, João grabbed him by the arm. "José, I need to talk with you." And he told him all about his research in the crime scene area. Everywhere there were well-marked footsteps. And in some places there were signs of superficial digging. His thinking was that someone had buried something there, whatever it was, and now was coming back to retrieve it, possibly at night.

"Stop!" José cut him off.

"Stop? Why?"

"Stop!" José insisted in a particularly severe tone of voice.

João didn't reply at first. What could account for his brother's determined attitude? So he inquired.

"It's better for us not to get involved," José responded. And he said nothing more.

* * *

Tó-Zé woke up his father. "Father, someone's in the courtyard. Listen."

Santarém jumped up and made a sign to his son not to make any noise. "Look through the window. I'll go around the house."

With a heavy stick in his hand, he left by the back door. He heard a rustle and the sound of footsteps running away. "Hey, you bastard! Show your face!" Santarém shouted.

The sounds of the retreating intruder faded away. The silence and darkness seemed to enlarge the space. Tó-Zé joined his father and they both stood there wordlessly guessing at the night's secret.

This was something new. Someone spying on them at night? Who could it be? What could they want?

Something new also happened with João. When he headed, as usual, toward the pine forest, he realized he was being followed. Maneuvering himself between walls and bushes, and peering back, surprisingly, he seemed to recognize Ernesto the barkeep as his pursuer. He turned around and hastened back home.

"What would he want?" João asked his brother, telling him about the incident.

"Either he wants to uncover a charge against us, or he's afraid we might uncover something against him."

"I don't understand," João admitted.

With redoubled caution, he continued going to the pine forest and bringing wildflowers to his nieces. But signs of his growing anxiety were visible. He had a peculiar way of gathering flowers. Beyond searching for them, he scratched the terrain at the crime scene and all around it.

One day, when he returned from the spot, very nervous, he found his brother and seized his arm. "Don't tell me it was you?" he asked.

"Nonsense," José Afonso answered, understanding what his brother was insinuating. "You're crazy. Who put that idea in your head?"

"Tell me, José," he insisted. "Tell me it wasn't you."

"No, it wasn't me," he replied calmly. "Stay calm."

"If it was you and they discovered it, what would happen to your children and all of us? Pardon me, but listen, if it was you, I'd do anything for them not to discover you. Anything, believe me."

"And I, too, would help you in anything if it was you," said José.

Hearing these words, João removed from his pocket two cartridges and the pistol's cartridge clip, exactly what he had picked up that first day at the crime scene.

Uncharacteristically, José lost his patience. "Throw that away!"

"Away? Why? If it was yours, I would have thrown it away already. This way they can discover the murderer."

"Throw it away, and don't cause trouble," José demanded.

"I'm not causing anything. Now I'm telling you: stay calm."

And, returning the cartridges and the clip to his pocket, he walked away. José stayed a few more moments, annoyed and pensive.

* * *

Without warning, Sanches from Judiciary reappeared in town, bearing big news. It turned out that Santarém had not emigrated to France for a year, as he had said. The whole time he was absent from the village he spent in Lisbon—in prison.

The record of the police questioning, and of the court case, all these documents now having come to light, explained everything.

He owed a lot of money to Vargas and, as Vargas had notified him to pay immediately, otherwise he would confiscate his assets and take possession of his rental lands, Santarém had sent him a letter threatening to kill him if he tried to put those threats into effect. "You can be certain I will kill you!" There it was in black and white. Vargas took him to court, he was sentenced and imprisoned for a year before returning to the village.

Sanches said he had given this information only to the GNR sergeant, who later swore he never passed it along to anyone. But somehow or other this news raced all through town, and then the Gertrudes sisters spread it in their own fashion.

"Ay, girl," said one, "what that man is capable of doing! There's only one thing I don't understand, though. Dona Alzira insists it was José Afonso, but by the looks of things it might well have been Santarém."

"And why not both?" said the other. "It would be good to find out if they ever meet. Since they live close to each other, it wouldn't be hard to keep an eye on them."

Gossip, rumor, talk all ran through the village. There were mysteries and suspicions galore. Sanches himself was confused.

One time, when he was walking with the sergeant, he saw Pinto the coalman emerging toward them in the distance and then suddenly turning back. Sanches reacted. "Why is that guy evading us?"

He's not evading, the sergeant explained. He was always like that, a fraidy-cat.

"Where does he live? Sanches inquired.

"He shows up in the village from time to time, sells his coal and disappears."

"But where does he live?" Sanches repeated.

Really, no one knew. Undoubtedly in some shack high up in the mountains. Nothing more than that was known.

"Curious," Sanches reflected. "It wouldn't be a bad idea to detain him."

"It wouldn't be easy," the sergeant replied.

Newly intrigued by this incident, Sanches decided to immediately proceed with his investigation and, as planned, to visit the Manor once again.

He drove his car up to the gate, saying he wished to speak with the mistress. As before, she received him impatiently and angrily.

Brites followed close behind, as if to protect her from any aggression.

"So they're finally going to bring him to court? Fine. But what are they waiting for?"

Yes, for sure they would bring José Afonso to court, Sanches explained, but he needed some additional information from the estate.

"What information? And be quick about it, I don't have time."

"Do you know of anyone who owed money to your husband?"

"Tell him, Brites, tell him, so he'll leave us in peace. Tell him."

Brites said that as far as Santarém and José Afonso were concerned, neither appeared to have owed Vargas any money. They had already paid up their debts. But there were many others who owed, some of them rather considerable sums.

"Who?"

"I'd have to take a better look at the books."

Sanches said goodbye, remarking that he was going to the tavern to gather more information.

"Him, for example, Ernesto," Brites explained. "He owed Vargas a lot of money and still owes it to the estate."

"We'll soon find out," Sanches said as he left.

* * *

Sanches went to the bar. As he did the first time, he crossed the full house, heading straight for the counter, and asked for a glass.

"What's this jerk doing here again?" a loud, rebellious voice was heard.

"Checking out the soles of our boots," someone guffawed.

Also, like the first time, Ernesto welcomed him amiably, as if forgetting the ridiculous spectacle from the last visit.

"A pleasure to see you here again." And without pausing for Sanches to initiate the conversation, he added, "Have you looked at the soles of all the boots in the village? Have you found the killer?"

"It won't be long before we find him," Sanches responded, pretending not to pick up on the insolence and the humor. "Now I would like to obtain some further information."

"Go ahead," Ernesto encouraged him.

"In the days since I was here last—anything new?"

Yes, there was lots of news. Everyone suspected everyone. And overall, there was much confusion.

"And how's business? Lots of people as always—"

"It's going well, as you see. It's always the same customers, but everyone fits in."

Keeping in mind what Brites had told him, Sanches proceeded. "Money coming in, I see. But are there debts, too?"

Ernesto hesitated in his response, and Sanches went into attack mode. "Do you have debts or not?"

"Yes, a few."

"Did you owe anything to Vargas?"

"Yes, something."

"A lot or a little?"

"Something—"

"If you don't want to say, don't say. But it would be better if you said."

Ernesto composed his thoughts. "A lot of people around here owed him."

"Naturally," Sanches commented, and then went quiet.

"I don't understand," said Ernesto. "It seems the only piece missing now is being considered a suspect myself."

"It's not missing by much," Sanches replied—and left.

In town he met with the sergeant. "This is more complicated than it appeared. I just came for a quick visit, but I have to go back to Central."

"You know, Senhor Sanches," said the sergeant, "there's nothing more to be done with this case. You're not going to solve anything. That's the way it is, and that's the way it will remain."

"It will not remain," answered Sanches.

"Or it will," the sergeant spoke back. "Someone fired the shots. But it was the whole village that killed Vargas."

* * *

The sergeant received the latest news. Judiciary Central would not accept that this crime go unpunished.

However, it was now no longer Sanches but one Oliveira charged with furthering the investigation. He appeared at the GNR post and sought out the sergeant. "I'm Agent Oliveira from Judiciary. I read Sanches's report, he spoke to me about you, and I would like you to continue helping us."

The sergeant shrugged his shoulders. He believed the matter closed, and it did not seem to him there was anything more to be done.

Oliveira believed otherwise. There were many new angles to try. Look—Sanches above all attempted to establish where the suspects were at the time of the crime and the motives that might have led to it.

But one essential thing had evaded him: knowing who had face-to-face encounters with Vargas, how often, for what reason and where. "This is what we also have to establish if we want to find the culprit."

Contradicted, the sergeant agreed they would have to return to the homes of the principal suspects.

"No," Oliveira said, "now we're going to summon them to come to the post and the interrogations will take place here."

"Aren't you considering going to the Manor?" asked the sergeant.

"It would be useless," Oliveira answered. "Sanches's report doesn't need more information."

The first summoned to the post was Santarém. He had reasons to complain, and they were serious. He confirmed the observations that Sanches had made. He had asked for a loan of money from Vargas, with the collateral of lands he possessed. And after Vargas had threatened him with taking the lands, Santarém had written him a letter threatening him with death. He was sentenced, spent a year away from the village, and when he returned, Vargas had assumed control of a good portion of the lands.

"A good motive to kill him, no?" Oliveira commented. "And where did you meet with him?"

Santarém responded promptly. "Always at the Manor, next to the front gate."

"We'll see."

"You just have to go and ask," he said rudely, "or would you like me to take you there and introduce you?"

There's nothing to be done with this guy, Oliveira thought, and he sent him away.

The second to be summoned to the post was Ernesto the barkeep. In the last conversation he had with him, Sanches caught him in omissions and contradictions. He appeared nervous and insecure.

Yes, he confirmed what he had said to Sanches. That he did owe Vargas some money and that Vargas was demanding payment.

Oliveira restated Sanches's question. "A lot or a little?"

"Moderate."

"A lot or a little?"

"Moderate."

Oliveira seemed satisfied with his response. "All right. And where did you meet?"

Ernesto paused a moment, finally saying, "At the tavern."

"Vargas at the tavern? Now this is news."

"At the tavern, and at the counter. You can ask."

Oliveira directed the question to the sergeant. "Vargas at the tavern? This sounds like a whopper of a story. I don't see any record that he had ever gone there."

The third to appear at the post was José Afonso. Oliveira recited the accusations against Vargas. His daughter Gabriela going to work there as a housemaid, Vargas having abused the little girl, his moving boundary lines on the estate, and occupying lands his family had been renting.

"Good motive to kill him, don't you think?" said Oliveira ironically, as he had done with Santarém.

The response was unexpected. "Yes, more than enough motives."

"Do you understand the gravity of what you just said?"

"Yes, I do. I didn't say I killed him nor that I would, but there were motives for it." And setting aside his normal even keel, he added, "And if it was you, Senhor, and your daughter, what would you think and do?"

Oliveira didn't react to that and went on with his questioning. "Where did you meet with him?"

José's tone returned to normal. "Once I went up to the Manor, when I went to fetch Gabriela. Other times in the village in front of my house."

"I see, Sergeant," Oliveira remarked after the last suspect had left, "our interrogations didn't produce results. We have to find another way."

* * *

João did not heed his brother's orders and warnings. As always, along the way to the forest, he stopped to see if anyone was following him. And once more, this happened. Looking back, he saw a figure hiding himself. He resolved to see who it was. As he approached, the figure got up and fled. Even from a distance, by his stature, his gait, and the glow of his hair, he recognized Ernesto the taverner. This was the second time he had followed him.

Again taking an extra measure of care, he returned to the scene several times, but didn't notice being followed, and he continued his investigation.

He altered his schedule. Sometimes around lunch time, other times midafternoon, and sometimes at twilight. Each time he went, the land revealed ever deeper signs of being probed.

He shifted his focus now from trying to uncover whatever it was that was buried, to trying to surprise the unknown person who went there to that end.

Noting his brother's strange absences, José repeated what he had earlier said to him. "João, don't get us mixed up in this business." But João paid no mind.

One day he decided to go to the scene at night, telling his brother he was going to the bar for a drink. "I believe this is the first time you're going there," José observed. "I repeat: Don't get us mixed up in this business."

João went to the bar. He had a glass of wine at the counter, as though nothing had happened with Ernesto. Many looked at him, surprised. Ernesto served him without comment, but with a questioning look. And the crowd, amazed to see him there, were even more astonished when they saw him suddenly get up and leave.

Halting every so often to check if he was being followed, he approached the crime scene as usual. Complete silence reigned in the pine forest. In the dense shadows, he didn't see the trunks of the trees, so much as imagine them.

Patiently, João placed himself at a certain distance behind some low bushes. The long wait, the darkness and the silence made the mystery and anxiety even more profound.

Lo and behold, not far off, the light of a lantern shone. The light rocked back and forth, then stopped. João could see the legs lighted by the lantern the intruder put on the ground. Cutting through the night came the clang of metal attacking the ground.

It stopped, the lantern went out, and in a nearby spot, the lantern went on again to the repeated sound of excavation.

Then, again, darkness and silence, for several minutes, and then nothing more. Whoever it was had certainly departed.

The next morning, João left early and, despite his lame leg, ran as fast as he could to see the evidence of the excavations. They weren't deep, but were numerous, wider than before and in no pattern.

Back at the house, he told his brother the reason for his unsettled state and shared what he had witnessed the previous night. He confirmed that someone was going around the scene of the crime looking for whatever it was that was buried. The earth showed fresh signs of disturbance, and the number and irregularity of the diggings showed a growing, restless nervousness.

"You told me once you'd help me. Are you ready for this?"

Yes, now José was inclined to help, even if he didn't much believe they would succeed. With that decided, the brothers headed to the locale the next evening. From a distance, they saw lights in the forest—a lantern and movement.

"We have to seize whoever it is. But doing it just the two of us, unarmed, could be dangerous."

Who else could go with them? Matias the carpenter, José remembered. He was a brave man.

But that wouldn't work either. The unknown man had to be taken into custody on the spot.

Following that determination, they went to the GNR post in the town to speak with the sergeant. From the start he was incredulous. "What do you want? The case is closed. The person you saw could just be someone collecting pine needles."

João then explained everything he had observed. No question about it, this guy was not there to gather pine needles, but to find something buried near the scene of the crime.

"All right," the sergeant ended up agreeing.

João had devised a plan. "We have to arrive beforehand and hide ourselves in the bushes. If we arrive when he's already there, he'll see us and will have time to escape."

Game for the operation, the sergeant enthusiastically expanded the plan. If the unknown person is searching for something buried, we have to seize him just as he's finding it. We'll be hiding, but we can only attack when we finally see he has achieved his objective. And we'll repeat the operation until we grab him in the act.

They established some details. "If not the first time, if necessary we'll go repeated times and wait. It's safer. You, as you propose, can bring Matias the carpenter with you. Agreed. And I will bring one of my young soldiers. Whoever it is, we won't let him escape."

*   *   *

They arrived at the site an hour and a half after nightfall. They spread out, leaving free the area leading from the road.

On one side were José Afonso and Matias the carpenter, who agreed to offer his help. On the other, the sergeant, the young GNR soldier, and lame João. By agreement, the GNR would attack whoever appeared. But it would be João, who knew the unknown man's maneuvers, who would decide the moment of attack.

The first, and the second night, the scene was the same: the lantern, the pacing back and forth from one side to the other, the noise of excavation. But the intruder ended up leaving without what he wanted.

Departing from the locale, the sergeant could not hold back. "It's not working. There's no reason for continuing like this. We can go one more time, but we don't expect he'll take anything out of the ground. Let's seize him to find out who it is and what he's searching for."

That idea met with opposition, but in the end they did agree. João insisted, and he won the argument, that he would continue to be the one to decide the moment of attack.

"If the next time we see nothing and we don't grab the guy," the sergeant said, "I'm not coming back. You do what you want."

Two days later, once again in the silent peace of night, the time grew ever longer and the group waited. They held out, anxious with uncertainty over nabbing or missing their target, and anguished over the likely uselessness of their effort.

One more hour? Two more? Patiently waiting was unbearable. When would the mystery be revealed? Minutes seemed like hours.

Finally the moment arrived.

Not far from where they were ensconced, a lantern and a figure were moving.

"Now?" the sergeant asked in a low voice.

"Shhhh," João hissed. And they waited for another anxious few minutes.

They heard the noise of metal in the earth. The movement and the sound repeated themselves several times.

"Do we attack?" the sergeant asked again.

"Shhhh," João demanded, holding back the sergeant's arm.

Finally, the figure bent over one more time, and by the light of the lantern they could see him clearly removing something from the ground.

"Now!" said João. They ran.

"Halt!" the sergeant shouted, advancing in a single jump. "Hands in the air!"

The intruder's lantern went out, and the GNR soldier's lantern now lit up the scene. There, close by, apparent even in the darkness, was the figure of a man holding a shovel.

Everything happened fast. The man was subdued. They took a small, but heavy bundle from his hands and led him out to the road, shoved along by José Afonso and Matias the carpenter.

There, a car with its lights off was parked. Only there could they clearly see his face, and were they shocked! It was Brites, the employee at the Manor.

Brites quickly composed himself. "What do you men want with me? Give me the package and leave me in peace."

"You want the pistol you were looking for. Don't even think about it," said João, touching the package.

"Don't let him escape!" the sergeant shouted to his soldier. "Secure him good!"

He withdrew a few steps with José Afonso, João and Matias the carpenter, trying to figure out what to do with the man.

"He's detained, and must continue to be," said José Afonso. "And taken to town and put in the lockup. Then hand him over to Judiciary."

"Right," the sergeant agreed. "We'll take him, but you go there tomorrow for a first deposition."

That's what was done. From the GNR post, he was taken to the town jail. It was left to Sanches, whom the sergeant called in for the job, to interrogate the prisoner.

"I never suspected it was you. But the drama is over. You will spill the whole truth, like it or not. Even if we stay here the rest of our lives, you will spill it all in the end."

With only short breaks, the questioning lasted several days and nights. The prisoner resisted as long as he was able, but wound up confessing to the crime.

With Vargas dead, and given both the responsibilities he had already assumed and his relationship with Dona Alzira, he would be left to rule the estate. He planned the crime. He persuaded Vargas to go to the estate's pine forest at night under the pretext of going there to catch some thieves stealing trees from his forest.

But at the site, nerves set in. They stepped out of the car and walked into the forest in the dark.

"So?" Vargas inquired impatiently. "This isn't the pine forest on my estate."

"Let's catch them over here on this side," said Brites in a trembling voice.

A few more steps and then silence. There was no sign or sound of cutting any trees.

Vargas turned doubtful. "What kind of foolishness is this?" And he started to go for Brites. But Brites jumped back, and shaking suddenly with a shiver, he pulled the trigger and shot. Three times. Once, again, and again, in the chest, to be sure he wouldn't live.

Vargas fell, and Brites felt confused. He quickly buried the pistol, took his time on the return road, and went back to the Manor on foot. At the front gate, before entering, he tried to regain his composure and present himself at the house as though he had never left.

He left the car where it was so that people would assume it was Vargas who left it there before entering the pine forest.

A complete confession.

*　*　*

Brites's trial at the town court was a grand event for the village. People rushed to attend it.

Only a disinterested José Afonso went on with his day-to-day life.

It was just the opposite with Santarém. During those days he exhibited a remarkable joyousness, spouting out his commentary on every aspect of the case.

Clotilde, of course, remembered what her husband had told her. "Relax. The police will never discover it." He had sworn to himself only to speak of "it" once they had found the killer. Now the time had come for an explanation.

On the eve of the crime, Santarém received a threat from Vargas. Either immediately pay what he owed, or Vargas would take the best lands. Their face-to-face encounter took place at the Manor gate.

Though they spoke in hushed voices, there was a moment in the argument when Vargas got excited. "If you didn't learn anything the last time, you will learn this time."

Santarém answered, "The last time it was you who fucked with my life. This time it will be me who fucks with yours."

If this encounter and the subject of their conversation, shortly before the crime occurred, had ever become known, it would have been difficult to escape an accusation against him as the perpetrator.

The memory made him laugh. "So it's like I told you, Clotilde, they'd never discover it."

Now he attended every session of the trial. He arrived arrogantly before the courtroom door was opened, seated himself in the very front row of chairs, and attentively followed the hearing. More than once the judge threatened to expel him from the room if he did not cease making remarks out loud—always aggressive and discourteous toward the defendant, toward Vargas and toward the court.

In a break between sessions, he met Sanches in the corridor. Standing in front of him, he practically forced him to stop. "How's it going, Senhor Sanches? I see they wound up finding the culprit."

Sanches tried to get away without responding to the provocation, but Santarém detained him for another minute. "Congratulations, Senhor Sanches, congratulations."

The agent managed to get away. He had barely gone a few steps, however, before he turned back. "If it wasn't this one, it will be another. Nothing is lost in delay. Don't forget it."

Lame João, witness for the prosecution, maintained a rather different attitude and offered fundamental details in explaining the crime.

In the courtroom, he looked askance at Sanches and Oliveira, who testified as the investigators and were praised by the court. His expression was passive, and he made no deprecatory comments. But, conscious of the role he played in the discovery of the criminal, he acted indifferently toward other people's attitudes.

Ernesto the barkeep kept spinning around in his social whirl. He talked with everyone, gathered opinions and in a whisper, almost in secret, spread false notions and claptrap.

The Gertrudes sisters couldn't not be there. But from the village to the town was a stretch too far for their ancient legs. They fell into luck, though: On the road, Ernesto the barkeep was driving a carriage and stopped.

"Aunties! If you're going to town, I'll help you get up onboard. I'm also going to the trial."

With some awkwardness they got up onto the carriage, sat down next to Ernesto and vainly adjusted their colorful kerchiefs. They stepped down in the courthouse square.

"Good luck, aunties. We'll see you later." And he rode away.

He circulated about, asked questions of everybody, and went around making up sensationalistic stories. On his way back in the carriage, he once again met the Gertrudes sisters. "Hey, aunties. I'll take you, get on board, here, let me help you."

And once again they seated themselves by his side, very erect and arranging their kerchiefs.

Along the way, Ernesto never stopped talking. "That's the way it goes, aunties. Do you remember that encounter we had?"

"We couldn't forget it, Senhor Ernesto."

"As you see, I was right. Do you remember I told you who the killer was?"

"Haah!" the old ladies exclaimed in shock, because he had told them the culprit was José Afonso. Conversation stopped there.

At the end of the trial, the courtroom emptied, but not everything was finished. Pinto the coalman entered, took a few steps in, stopped for a minute to look around, and left—as always, like a mysterious fugitive.

After so many false judgments, after so many suspects and unfounded accusations, the village felt liberated from a terrible tension, from a miasma of ill will and enmities.

Brites was sentenced to fifteen years in prison. No one in the village spoke of him anymore.

The situation at the estate brought new developments. Dona Alzira, who for some time already had presented signs of mental decline, went crazy. Completely. She spent part of her days—and nights—shouting, and had. violent episodes. She threw her china to the floor, railing at the housemaids. She tore up the curtains claiming to rearrange them. And one day, in a fit, she smashed the mirror in front of which she was combing her hair.

The staff were afraid and several of them, men and women both, deserted the Manor and went to work in town.

Relatives of Vargas appeared, placed her in a psychiatric hospital, and took charge of the estate.

The situation then gained a certain new normalcy. Staff were rehired. Agricultural work started up again. Relations between the owners of the estate and the people of the village returned in essence to what they had been in Vargas's time. The new landlords furthered their attempt to appropriate the smallholders' lands. The miserable wages continued. The debt peonage continued. Abuses and threats continued.

Now, however, the estate owners displayed a bit more prudence with their personnel and the smallholders. Everyone, in their own way, took past experience into account, trying to avoid provoking—in the unspoken consciousness of the people—motives to murder.

* * * * *

Photo: Eduardo Gageiro

A short biographical note on the author

Manuel Tiago

Manuel Tiago was the pen name of Álvaro Cunhal. Edições Avante! in Lisbon, has published nine titles by Manuel Tiago: *Até amanhã, camaradas* (Until Tomorrow, Comrades), which was adapted as a Portuguese television series in 2005; *A estrela de seis pontas* (The Six-Pointed Star); *A casa de Eulália* (Eulália's House); *Fronteiras* (Border Crossings); *Um risco na areia* (A Line in the Sand); *Os corrécios e outros contos* (The Slackers and Other Stories); *Sala 3 e outros contos* (The 3rd Floor and Other Stories); and *Lutas e vidas* (Struggle and Life). *Cinco dias, cinco noites* (Five Days, Five Nights), adapted to film in 1996, was the first of his works of fiction to appear in English. In its continuing series of Manual Tiago books, International Publishers has so far released *Five Days, Five Nights*, *The Six-Pointed Star*, and now *The 3rd Floor and Other Stories of the Portuguese Resistance*.

Álvaro Cunhal was born in Coimbra, Portugal, on November 9, 1913. He began his revolutionary activity as a student at the law school (Faculdade de Direito) of Lisbon. He participated in the student movement and was elected in 1934 as the student representative to the University Senate. He was a militant in the Federation of Portuguese Communist Youth (Federação da Juventude Comunista Portuguesa), and was elected its secretary-general in 1935. In that year he went underground and participated in Moscow in the Sixth International Communist Youth Congress. He joined the Portuguese Communist Party (Partido Comunista Português, PCP) in 1931.

Arrested in 1937 and 1940, and subjected to torture, he returned to political struggle as soon as he was freed after several months in prison. He participated in the reorganization of the PCP in the early 1940s. Again living clandestinely, he was a member of the party Secretariat from 1942 to 1949.

Arrested anew in 1949 and brought before a fascist court, he delivered a ringing denunciation of the fascist dictatorship and a defense of his party's program. Judged guilty, he remained for 11 years in fascist prisons, almost eight of them in complete isolation. On January

3, 1960, he escaped from the prison fortress at Peniche together with a group of brave communist militants. Once again called to the Secretariat of the Central Committee, he was elected Secretary General of the PCP in 1961.

Living abroad, in Moscow and Paris, from that time forward he participated in numerous congresses and gatherings with communist parties and other revolutionary forces in international conferences. He played a critical role in organizing worldwide support, especially within the socialist countries, for the independence movements in the far-flung Portuguese colonies in Africa.

After the downfall of the fascist dictatorship on April 25, 1974, he served as Minister without Portfolio in the first four provisional governments, and was elected as a deputy to the Constituent Assembly in 1975 and to the Assembly for the Republic in 1975, 1979, 1980, 1983, 1985 and 1987. He was a member of the Council of State from 1982 to 1992.

In accordance with the decisions made at the 14th Congress of the PCP in 1992 concerning renewal and a new structure of leadership, he stepped down as Secretary General of the PCP and was elected by the Central Committee as President of the National Council of the party.

In December 1996, the 15th Congress of the PCP eliminated the National Council of the party and its presidency. Cunhal was re-elected as a member of the Central Committee.

He was re-elected to the Central Committee at the 16th and 17th party congresses in December 2000 and November 2004 respectively.

Under his own name Cunhal published several books about politics. He was a gifted artist as well: A book of his collected drawings has appeared. In addition, he published an original translation of Shakespeare's *King Lear*.

He died at the age of 91 on June 13, 2005. His funeral in Lisbon was attended by half a million people. He had one daughter, Ana Cunhal. The Portuguese government issued a postage stamp in his memory and later, in 2021, another stamp commemorating the centennial of the PCP to which he had devoted his life.

About the Translator

ERIC A. Gordon, a Los Angeles resident since 1990, is a native of New Haven, Connecticut. His undergraduate degree is from Yale University, where he majored in Latin American Studies. He studied Spanish five years and Portuguese two years. He also took a summer residency in Portuguese at New York University. He went on to Tulane University, where he continued studying Portuguese and wrote a master's thesis on the opera in Rio de Janeiro in the 19th century, using original sources uncovered in the Arquivo Nacional. He earned a doctorate in history, also from Tulane, writing his dissertation about the anarchist movement in Brazil in the pre-World War I era. He also studied Portuguese language and culture under a Gulbenkian Foundation fellowship in Lisbon.

International Publishers initiated its Manuel Tiago series in 2020 with Gordon's translation of *Five Days, Five Nights*, followed by *The Six-Pointed Star*, and now *The 3rd Floor*. When complete, the series will comprise all nine works of fiction by Álvaro Cunhal, each appearing for the first time in English.

Gordon is the author of *Mark the Music: The Life and Work of Marc Blitzstein*, and co-author of *Ballad of an American: The Autobiography of Earl Robinson*. A memoir in short story form that he translated from Portuguese, *Waving to the Train and Other Stories*, by Hadasa Cytrynowicz, appeared in 2013 from Blue Thread Press. In 2015 he executive produced the compact disk *City of the Future: Yiddish Songs from the Former Soviet Union*, a collection of songs composed in 1931 by Samuel Polonski to the lyrics of major Soviet Yiddish poets. He is the author of a currently unpublished political autobiography.

From 1995 to 2010, Gordon was Director of the Workers Circle/Arbeter Ring in Southern California. He previously worked at Social and Public Art Resource Center, helping to produce murals all around the city of Los Angeles, which gave him the experience to commission a mural at the Workers Circle building. He was Southern California Chapter Chair of the National Writers Union (Local 1981 UAW/AFL-CIO) for two terms. He has written for dozens of local, national, and international publications, mostly about art, music, culture, and politics. From 2014 onward, he has been a staff writer and editor for *People's World* online newspaper.

From 2006-09 Gordon took coursework toward certification as a Secular Jewish Leader, referred to in Yiddish as a *vegvayzer*. Upon graduation, he became a legal officiant certified to conduct weddings and other ceremonial functions, a role equivalent in law to a minister, priest, or rabbi. He has a similar endorsement as a Humanist celebrant for people of any background. For five years he served as a Deputy Commissioner of Civil Marriage for the County of Los Angeles, where he conducted 1500 marriages.

Eric Gordon can be contacted at ericarthurgo@gmail.com.

Questions to Ponder and Discuss

An Uncommon Education

At the end of "An Uncommon Education," Miguel and Sofia will operate a safe house outside of Lisbon. It's a far stretch from Sofia's romantic homey fantasy. Will this be a satisfying life for the couple, without jobs and careers? How do you imagine their future?

Miguel seems like a young man with no special passion, interests or ambition. Did he have any real alternative in life? Was he backed by his indecisiveness into the solution António Pereira proposed? Might he have had a better life emigrating from Portugal?

The author creates so much mystery around the life and behavior of Miguel's father Midões. What do you think he did for a living?

The 3ʳᵈ Floor

The author includes a number of questionable characters amongst the prison population in "The 3ʳᵈ Floor." There's Karl, the supposed Jewish German aviator, there's the two Polish officers, and the banker Vernstein. Who are they really, and what is their significance in the story?

Was it hard for you to believe that the sawing of the window bars could proceed without drawing any attention from the other prisoners? Or were you willing to go along with this in your generous "suspension of disbelief?"

Struggle and Life

In "Struggle and Life," Constança clearly loved Leonel. But just as clearly, she did not know what she was getting into entering the underground life with him. Did Leonel really love her, or was she mostly just a bed partner, as she finally came out and said?

He placed his political responsibility above his personal life. Was this simply an unavoidable necessity, or could they have worked things out another way?

How is their relationship different from Miguel and Sofia's in the first story? Are there comparable conditions today where activists are forced to make those kinds of choices?

There are some women comrades, like Joana and Marisa, but the author does not assign them much importance in the story. Do you think that merely reflects the reality of political life at that time and place, or would you have liked to see a more prominent female character in the story?

This story features a lot of party meetings! What do you think about the way they were conducted? Were they old-fashioned and perhaps rather hierarchical, or even if so, was that a valid and efficient— perhaps even timeless—way to run a meeting and make decisions? Would you have done differently?

The Vargas Case

In "The Vargas Case," did you guess who the killer was? If so, how soon, and what was your tipoff? If you were convinced it was someone else, why? Yet, if you reread the early passages about the killer, the clues are certainly there. How did you overlook them?

Ernesto the barkeep is an ambiguous character. He gladly circulated Dona Alzira's opinion that José Afonso was the killer, and then he was observed following João to the murder scene. What was his motivation for these behaviors?

www.ingramcontent.com/pod-product-compliance
Lightning Source LLC
Chambersburg PA
CBHW030531020726
47494CB00004B/1304